© **Copyright 2019 by Dangerous Liaisons Books - All rights reserved.**

In no way is it legal to reproduce, duplicate, or transmit any part of this document in either electronic means or in printed format. Recording of this publication is strictly prohibited and any storage of this document is not allowed unless with written permission from the publisher. All rights reserved.

Respective authors own all copyrights not held by the publisher.

This book is a work of fiction. Names, characters, places and incidents are either the product of the author's imagination or are used fictionally. Any resemblance to actual persons, living or dead, or to actual events or locales is entirely coincidental.

A Foreign Affair

Table of Contents

Introduction 3
Chapter 1. Concerning a Certain Eligible Young Woman 5
Chapter 2. First Stop on the Grand Tour 15
Chapter 3. Paris, City of Light 45
Chapter 4. Transalpine Trek 73
Chapter 5. Touring Turin and Venetian Adventures 88
Chapter 6. Venice 94
Chapter 7. The Zanes 114
Chapter 8. The Cad 151
Chapter 9. Letters from Away 164
Chapter 10. The Lost Dress 208
Chapter 11. The Grand Ball 213
Chapter 12. After the Ball 238
Chapter 13. Letters from Abroad 251
Chapter 14. An Encounter on a Coach 258
Chapter 15. A Package in the Post 272
Chapter 16. A Stranger in Our Midst 291
Chapter 17. A Stroll in the Garden 302
Chapter 18. Return to the Baying Hounds 313
Chapter 19. Days of Turmoil 329
Chapter 20. The Entourage 340
Chapter 21. The Wedding 350

Lisa Brooks

Introduction

How can an eligible young lady in the 1818 season be expected to find a suitable husband? This was the riddle that wealthy Lady Emma Shaftesbury was wrestling with as she looked over the crop of young dandies who had attended this season's balls. She felt strongly that it was important she see the world before she married, and her mother agreed, deciding to take her on The Grand Tour, first to France, where she sees the beauty of the fashion world and, with luck, her future wedding dress, and then to Italy where she would experience great art and, possibly, true love.

In Italy, she meets Federico, an exotic Venetian nobleman, and falls head over heels for him. When her mother discovers her scandalous dalliance, she is horrified and forces a move, but Emma outwits her. She leaves a forwarding address to Federico, who writes to her and proposes marriage.

When she returns to England, he follows her and causes a stir at a ball by publicly declaring his love for her. However, custom dictates that he return to Italy to get his parents' permission. He leaves and is never heard from again.

Emma, humiliated, decides to re-enter the fray in London, but she no longer has the stomach for it. On her way back home by post coach, she meets another Italian gentleman, this one bound for France. When she tells him she will only marry a man who can buy her the dress she saw in a shop on the Champs Elysée, he accepts her challenge.

Will he rise to the occasion or turn out to be a cad? He is good friends with a well-known cad who is courting Emma's younger sister, so all signs point to disappointment. But nobody had counted on Emma's perseverance, strength of character, and ability to love. In the dazzling season in Regency England, Emma is one young lady you will never forget!

Chapter 1. Concerning a Certain Eligible Young Woman

"Mother," said Emma Shaftesbury in despair, looking over the gaggle of dandies who were gazing in her direction. "I am in the depths of despair about this predicament. You tell me I must marry or I shall become an old maid, and yet I should prefer to remain an old maid if I have to marry any of these buffoons."

"Emma!" said Anne Shaftesbury, her long-suffering mother. "You simply cannot speak that way of these gentlemen! They are the proud stock of our country's greatest leaders." She spoke these words, but in truth, she despaired of any of these young men becoming her sons-in-law as well.

"Mother, you know it is the singular duty of a young woman of this generation to marry well. Needless to say, the man I marry must be of irreproachable character, good social position, be frightfully well-off, and, above all, be devoted to me."

Emma Shaftesbury, twenty years of age and of good family, had never had cause to doubt that these were the same qualities she sought in a husband. "To be frank, I should be swept off my feet by any man who would just buy me a Paris gown," she said, imagining this to be the height of fashion in the post-Napoleonic world. Of course, Anne, her mother, knew she was given to off-hand quips and exaggeration, she could not help smiling at the thought.

Despite her advanced years for a spinster, Emma was finely formed in a singular sort of way - although she was excessively thin, she had a fine figure, (perhaps a trifle buxom), with an unruly, yet strangely beautiful mane of strawberry blonde ringlets, large blue eyes surrounded by long dark eyelashes, a small but charming upturned nose, full lips, good teeth, and small delicate hands unaccustomed to hard work, but familiar with the intricacies of the fortepiano. In short, had she been a prize horse, she would have fetched a good price.

What set Emma apart from the other marriageable young ladies was her highly adventurous soul, her desire to see the world and all its magnificence, and her insufferable inquisitiveness.

Her mother, Anne Shaftesbury, now in her forties and thus well-acquainted with the ways of the world, doted on her eldest daughter because she felt she was the most eligible, most eloquent, and most interesting thing she had ever had a hand in creating. Anne also had a younger daughter named Elizabeth, seventeen years of age, and still unready for marriage in the eyes of her doting father, the Baron Rufus Shaftesbury, Lord of Godington Manor in Kent, near Canterbury. Elizabeth showed a tendency toward inappropriate behavior and needed constant supervision. Their young son, Sebastian, was still only twelve years old, and seemed to be as bland as unsalted oatmeal.

"Oh mummy. I've been attending these blasted balls, dances, and gala events for nearly three years now. I almost dare not admit it, but do you not think perhaps I have outgrown Kent?"

The truth was, Anne was frightened to take her to the Capital. So much intrigue had been occurring in London, since the shocking assassination of Prime Minister Spencer Perceval and the fuss over the defeat of Napoleon, that Anne had begun to think of this palace intrigue as just more silly male concerns, and yet she knew there was no avoiding it. Consequently, she resolved to take Emma to be presented to society and to the Prince of Wales.

Even before they arrived, the city had been thrown into a pall when Princess Charlotte Augusta, daughter of the Prince of Wales, and current Princess of Wales, died right at the beginning of the season, during, they said, childbirth. Anne Shaftesbury had hoped that the birth of a royal baby would inspire her daughter to contribute to the family, but this unexpected and appalling shock threw her daughter into ever greater desire to be autonomous. Autonomy was not the sort of thing to be expected or even accepted among the young ladies of the gentry.

Despite this blot on the societal landscape, the season of 1817 and 1818 had all the requisite balls one would have expected. And as with every other season, all the eligible ladies attended, and some of the eligible gentlemen, along with some rakes and gadabouts attended, causing *billets doux* to be exchanged between young ladies and young marriageable bachelors.

Emma, having been presented to the Prince, dove into this activity with relish but, by the end of the season, although she had made many friends of the female persuasion, no young man had sufficiently distinguished himself that she felt the need to write to him upon her return to the manor. Nevertheless, she had mastered the dances - the Longways Country Dance, the Scotch Reel, the Cotillion, and the Quadrille, only stopping short of learning that scandalous new dance, the Waltz.

The fact of the matter was that young Emma Shaftesbury was more than usually clever, which was a distinct disadvantage for a young lady in good society at this time. When some handsome fop began pronouncing on the state of politics of which he may have had less than a passing acquaintance, Emma could not restrain herself from speaking her mind and correcting the young man's record. The dandyish young Earl of Houndsleigh, for example, had expounded on the folly of the democratic experiment in France.

"You thee," he lisped. "The ecthperiment in what our Gallic brethren have forgotten ith that the common folk have no love for order or good governanth. Mob rule ith theer folly in a thothiety tho temperamentally unfit for governanth."

Emma rolled her eyes at the Earl of Houndsleigh. "Surely you jest, your Lordship," she said. "For it has come to my attention that perhaps your Lordship himself is unfit for leadership owing to his unfortunate speech impediment."

Instantly, there was a stir in the group, and many young ladies moved noticeably away from Emma, although many of them noted (behind their fans, with a titter) that she had a point. Indeed, many of them had not understood the point the Earl had made, owing to the difficulty in comprehension that his lisp had caused.

Emma's powerful temper and rustic good looks endeared her to a good many young eligible brides but few young suitors. Suitors at this time were more concerned with preserving what society was left after the dear King George had gone mad. There were a few young men who found Emma's interpolations daring and clever, but these mealy-mouthed fellows dared not risk the ire of the foppish dandies who led good society at this time. Many of them feared the worst for their kind, and looked askance at those arrivistes who dared to enrich themselves through industry.

Although much of the Shaftesbury money had been made many years ago, Emma's father, Sir Rufus Shaftesbury, a Baron, had the effrontery to divest himself of his investments in silk, and invest in the hop industry.

"I know what people want, and it is certainly not silks. Not in this climate. We all need the same thing, and so good ale is the thing that shall line my pockets," he declared to his friends.

Although none of them dared mention this to him, several of them thought it a risky and dangerous investment for the betterment of society. "The lower classes are already too fond of their ale," said his friend and confidant, Sir Trevor Bowes. The issue of drink in the underclasses was a topic of great interest in the foppish class, and more than once, when a gentleman inquired about her family, Emma proudly told them that her father was a brewer of the hoppish beverage. "Daddy is a brewer," she would say, laughing. Affronted, these effete fops would dandily mince away, faw-fawing all the way, and never ask for a second dance, despite her exquisite form and skill in the art.

Over the course of the winter of her eighteenth year, Emma wrote voluminously to her many new friends scattered across England (and one, Fiona, in Fifeshire, Scotland), closely following the journey to matrimony of two of them. But for reasons that escaped Anne's notice, Emma wrote to no young men. Anne was not exactly in mourning about this - it is a sign of good character in a young lady to be choosey, she reasoned, and it would ensure her long-term happiness by making a well-considered choice at this critical time.

But Emma seemed to have lost herself in the wonders of the Continent and all the dashing figures of the swarthy race of Italians. She was forever reading the novels of Miss Fanny Burney, whose japes at the English aristocracy were still considered scandalous. Moreover, her love of the Continent and its men was poo-pooed by the members of English society who had failed to read Frances Burney's *Camilla*, preferring to find fault with what they did not know. This love of Fanny Burney inspired her mother Anne, in consultation with her father, Sir Rufus Shaftesbury, to take Emma on a journey of exploration: The Grand Tour. All this to provide her daughter with an opportunity to see the world and have a lifetime's worth of conversation.

Chapter 2. First Stop on the Grand Tour

"Nell!" called Emma from her bed chamber on the morning they were to leave. "Have you arranged to have my luggage taken?"

"I have seen to everything, Miss Emma," said Nell.

"I see," said Emma, slightly saddened to learn that there was nothing for her to do. "Then there is nothing to do but wait for the coach?"

"Precisely, Miss Emma. Just relax and enjoy the trip."

Emma's lady's maid, Nell, arranged for passage on a coach to take them to the port of Dover where they would embark for the perilous journey across the English Channel in late January. According to the very careful Nell, the coach that would take them there would depart from Canterbury and set off across the countryside, arriving three hours later, barring accidents (the thought of which discomfited Anne somewhat) at Dover. The fact was, this time of year was known in England as a time of inclement weather, when a bonnet could be ruined by a soaking if one were not circumspect in one's manner, to say nothing of soiling one's shoes and stockings, skirt, and petticoat. Emma had readily agreed to embark on this Grand Tour, as any young woman might, and, although Anne was not privy to Emma's inner thoughts, she felt she knew that the fascination with the Continent was something to be nurtured in her eldest daughter.

    Unbeknownst to Anne, Emma harbored a secret desire to be swept off her feet by an aristocratic mustachioed Italian, during one of the stops in this historically fascinating land. She frequently imagined herself being wooed in a piazza by a swarthy young gentleman who found her Englishness just as fascinating as she found his Italianness. She imagined the language barrier as a wall every bit as daunting as, but also as inspiring as the wall between Pyramus and Thisbe. She conjured up a masked ball in Venice, a parade of Pantalones, and a mysterious stranger depositing a beautifully written request for a meeting in her begloved hand. In truth, though, despite the studies with her governess in the French tongue and the intricacies of Italian, she was quite the neophyte when it came to continental manners.

After all, growing up at Godington Manor in Kent, she had become familiar with many of the rustic ways of the people and rarely encountered a well-bred stranger. Nevertheless, and perhaps because of this infrequency of encounter, foreigners were built up in her imagination, eclipsing all the qualities of the young Englishmen who might have been her suitors had she been less headstrong.

And yet, Emma was expected to find herself a suitor who would be of equal or superior rank to her father, who was a hereditary baron, and this was a difficult task for a young woman who was as self-sufficient as Emma. In truth, being a trifle dependent was seen as a good quality to London society, and Emma simply cared nothing for these artifices. She spoke her mind with a great deal of urgency when she felt the need. She recalled the conversation with the Earl of Harewood, expounding on the superiority of the English race, with his *bon mot* that "the continentals view their beard-splitters and borachios as gentlemen." She responded with remonstrations of her own where she observed that his Lordship seemed to be encumbered by the notion that all Europeans are without scruples, when in fact it was they, not us, who brought civilization to these shores.

"Would his Lordship not rather be ruled by the Magna Carta than by the ruffian King Harold?" She smiled and lowered her eyes in deference to his title if not his wit. Titters reverberated through the drawing room and it was noted that the Earl of Harewood was affronted by this indignity, particularly when Emma noted to her friends that she had feared he would, like Samson, tear down her repartee, since he was equipped with the self-same weapon: the jawbone of an ass!

For better or worse, Emma had developed something of a reputation for an acid tongue, and, although her mother was secretly proud of her daughter for this very quality, she knew she had to maintain a certain decorum in the higher echelons of society lest she be branded a "baggage." Anne had deftly navigated her way into good society and married well, but feared for her eldest daughter lest she be shunned.

"Emma," said Anne after the soirée in question. "One must remember one's place. You are a young girl and the Earl has had a wealth of experience on the continent. He served with Lord Nelson, you know."

"Yes, mother. I am aware that his lordship had experience in slaying Europeans, but I am not at all sure that such an experience qualifies one as a world traveler, nor as the Marco Polo of the Continent. Nor, in truth, does it offer enlightenment upon their characters, for a dead European has as little character as a dead Englishman, I dare say."

"Emma, I must remind you that such pronouncements are unbecoming in good society. You may win the battle but you'll surely lose the war. Please bear that in mind."

"Pshaw!" she exclaimed. "We shall go to visit these heathens and borachios and see if they are indeed the cads they are reputed to be. If they are, then I shall need an escort at all times."

Although she secretly admired her daughter's pluck, Anne decided that fighting her daughter on this issue was pointless; experience would teach her of her limitations. And with that, they embarked for the continent.

The night before they left Godington Manor, father held a soirée of the most genteel kind. He secured some of the most fashionable musicians to be found in London: a certain Mr. Salomon, a violinist, brought his chamber orchestra with him while Mr. Pleyel, a Frenchman and pianist was on hand to perform on the fortepiano (Emma's favorite instrument), and to accompany Miss Francesca Cuzzoni, an Italian songstress of rare skill and vocal dexterity to entertain the little coterie of friends and family. It was held in the ballroom of the manor, and the event, a sort of send-off for Miss Emma Shaftesbury, who, according to the invitation delivered by Ben, the errand boy, was going on a Grand Tour.

This gesture was considered very grand, perhaps overreaching, by the conservative ladies of the area. Tongues waggled for several weeks between the start of the Christmas season and their departure. Misses Merriweather and Wegg, the two unmarried ladies of the area who kept the lines of communication abuzz with their frenzied commentary on every eligible bachelor and spinster in the neighborhood, had much to say about the audacity of the headstrong Miss Emma Shaftesbury.

"She behaves like a young man when she is in good company," said Miss Wegg. "She argues and she sings without regard for the rules of decorum that dictate that a lady must be seen and not heard."

"Moreover, said Miss Merriweather, "this Miss Shaftesbury is wont to go out without a bonnet, her wild hair tousled by the weather and the wind, making her the shame of the county, and a caution to the young men who value their reputations."

Fortunately for Miss Shaftesbury, the Misses Merriweather and Wegg were scarcely paid attention to anymore. Their influence had peaked in the days of the Battle of Waterloo where Clarice Merriweather's brother Bruce (and Miss Annabelle Wegg's fiancé) had fought and died, and since he could not be brought back from the dead for another Waterloo, their influence had waned, with the result that Miss Shaftesbury was allowed to tramp through the county looking every bit the shock she was.

Despite these protestations from the roost, Emma and Anne Shaftesbury embarked on their journey in January 1818, on a day of foreboding grey clouds on the horizon of the western hills beyond.

In the coach bound for Dover, the two ladies were joined by several other ladies journeying to Dover to visit their ailing aunt, and a pair of young men who behaved as though they owned the conveyance.

"I say driver," one would shout to the driver. "Stop at this next post, would you? I must obey the call of nature."

"You-halloo, driver!" said the other. "Do be a good chap and allow me to buy some ale at the next post, won't you?"

They were delayed by more than an hour, much to the consternation of the Shaftesburys. Emma had insisted on bringing Nell, her lady's maid with her for the journey. Nell traveled, as was her custom, atop the carriage.

Anne abided the demands of these demanding gentleman without comment, secretly cursing them their brashness. After the first two stops, though, Emma lost patience with these two.

"Now see here, you louts," she said acidly. "If you need to stop so frequently, perhaps you should get out and walk, so as not to inconvenience the rest of the travelers."

Taken aback and much embarrassed, these two gentlemen apologized profusely and kept to themselves no doubt, Anne thought, preparing insults about her daughter. However, they kept their opinions to themselves, so as not to appear unchivalrous. The other ladies who were aboard, though, were impressed with Emma's resolve, and whispered their gratitude. As a result, the coach arrived in Dover by midday.

In Dover, Anne treated Emma to her last roast beef dinner before embarking on the ship to cross to Calais. Anne relished the tough native meat while Emma declared, "one thing I will not miss is the cuisine of my native isle. Indeed," she declared, "I hear that the leather in Italy is much tenderer than our English beef."

"Why Emma," said her mother. "Why ever do you speak of leather goods?"

"Because, maman," she said. "The English clearly feel the need to serve their leather with mashed potato and carrots."

Aboard the ship to the Continent, the ladies experienced the 'mal de mer' they had heard so much about. They had a little cabin berth in which to suffer, and Anne found herself incapacitated by the frightful issuance that befell sufferers of this ailment, while Emma appeared to be immune. She doted on her mother, and helped in myriad little ways to make the crossing more pleasant, but it took much longer than either of them had anticipated.

This channel crossing was supposed to take eighteen hours, and they had left at low tide, so as to make the trip that much swifter. However, twenty-two hours later, after they had consumed all the sandwiches Nell, her lady's maid, had made for them - they were, after all, a Kentish invention, the sandwich! - and after Anne had tamed her illness, took some air on the deck, nibbling on a ham sandwich proffered by her daughter.

Perhaps it was the salt of the ham, or just the salt air, but she recuperated in short order, and the remainder of the voyage was pleasant, with good head winds and a calm sea. Emma was permitted to discover the ship alone (with Nell, of course), and she made her way from pillar to post, examining everything with discernment. She was a good traveler, and was easily able to navigate her way around the boat before it landed at Calais. Indeed, she was the first to see land, and hollered to the dozing sailor in the crow's nest, "land ho!" much to the astonishment of the various gentlemen who had been eyeing her with suspicion.

Many of the men on the ship were foreigners, with Frenchmen making up the majority. Several of these gentlemen seemed to be the adventurous commoner types, as they wore caps that belied their common origins. Emma knew to avoid these sorts, although Nell found their company pleasant, as she reported afterward. As for Emma though, she avoided them as they were bound to take advantage. Still, she managed to find a pair of French gentlemen, who claimed they had spent several years in England during the reign of the Corsican.

Emma attempted to converse in French with them and found that she was relatively successful. The gentlemen, both of whom spoke perfect English, with scarcely the trace of an accent, complimented her on her command of the French tongue. Indeed, she was sufficiently emboldened by their blandishments that she continued to prattle on about the state of the French wine industry, charming the men with her knowledge. Unbeknownst to her, though, she was scandalizing the English ladies who had not the nerve to speak to strangers. And becoming aware of this teacup scandal, she went on and on, laughing with abandon and flirting shamelessly. The result was she had a wonderful time, while she caused others to have a wonderful time gossiping about her.

    She was spared the fruits of their labors by the landing of the ship. It was well past eleven in the morning, and they had been aboard for nearly a full day. Many of the elderly passengers, including her mother, had slept the night through, while the younger and more adventurous among them had braved the night winds of the Channel, and by the time the squat and unadventurous town of Calais came into view, many of them had no other thought in their heads than finding a hotel to rest up. Emma had a similar desire, having worn herself out with speaking French to the two Frenchmen.

    She hastened to find her mother as they came to shore, and her mother, revived by a long draught of *eau de vie*, was feeling very energetic.

"Do come along then Emma," said Anne. "Stay close to me, and I shall deal with these French."

"I say, mother," said an astonished Emma. "You seem uncharacteristically chipper this morning."

"It must be the sea air," said Anne. "But I feel like a schoolgirl!"

"It was the eau de vie," whispered Nell in Emma's ear.

"Oh my goodness!" she replied. "Does she not know it is a spirit?"

"Of course she does, but she chooses not to believe it. She had rather a lot of it in the cabin, and I suspect she is imbued with what the lower classes call 'liquid courage,'"

Emma laughed heartily to watch her mother lurch up the gangplank, nearly falling into the roiling water of the channel. Nell, true to form, held the inebriated Anne and saved her from herself and a watery grave.

Once she was on terra firma, she confidently commandeered a longshoreman, who lugged their baggage to a waiting carriage that was called a *diligence*.

"I say, chauffeur," she said confidently to the Frenchman sitting atop the diligence. "See voo play, troovay unn bun hotel." The bewildered Frenchman looked confused until Emma decided to try her hand and came off much better.

"Monsieur," she began. "Ma mère et moi sommes très fatigués après notre traversée de la Manche et nous aimerions trouver un bon hôtel dans la ville. Pourriez-vous s'il vous plaît nous emmener là-bas ?[1]"

"Ah oui, bien sûr, mademoiselle," said the Frenchman and whipping the horses, he set off toward the *Hotel Maurice* that lay on the Quai de la Loire. Nell, who, like her mistress, was somewhat brash in her delivery, took on the task of making sure that

---

[1] My mother and I are very tired after our voyage across the English Channel, and we would like to find a good hotel in the city. Could you please take us there?

they had adequate quarters in the slightly faded glory of the *Maurice*. They had a lovely room and both of the ladies were greatly refreshed for the long journey to Paris, which they planned to undertake the next day. The coachman, Benoit, who had conveyed them to the hotel, agreed to transport them to Paris for a reasonable fee that Nell was able to negotiate for them.

It must be said that this voyage had not been entered into without forethought. Sir Rufus had converted a quantity of their fortune into the francs that still bore the image of the Emperor, now languishing in St. Helena island off the coast of Africa. His imperial bearing was impressive to Emma, but revolting to Anne, who had read about his excesses in the many English periodicals of the time.

Nonetheless, thanks to the excellent service of Nell, who was now doing double duty as the lady's maid for both ladies, they were dressed and ready at nine in the morning after a breakfast of *croissants au beurre*, one of the most delicious pastries Emma had ever tasted. It was a simple bread-like delicacy, so delightfully flaky that she nearly abandoned the niceties of dining with cutlery and grasped it in her bare hands. Nell vowed that she would learn how to make this delightful pastry. And she was serious, right up until they boarded the *diligence* for Paris. Their driver, Benoit, told them that he would take them all the way to Paris, and that they would stop in Amiens at a fine inn, so that they would be refreshed for the journey to Paris. He had done this before, they concluded, and together they decided to put their trust in this honest workman.

In Amiens, he brought them to a fine-looking hotel and arranged for an excellent suite that provided a pair of down mattresses on stately beds, and a bathtub in the center of the room which neither of the ladies knew what to do with. They studied the white porcelain tub, commenting on the need for bathing that was a peculiarity of the French.

"Tis wonder they don't catch their death," said Anne in astonishment, to the wonder of her daughter.

"I don't think it's right, Ma'am," declared Nell as though she were looking at a bubbling cauldron filled with eye of newt and toe of frog. Emma, though, was entranced by this large tub, and inquired of the landlady, Madame Mortier, as to the purpose of this peculiar boudoir item, and the lady of the hotel informed her that it was primarily for young ladies who wanted to cleanse themselves before or after a "rendezvous." Emma returned to her mother, and informed her, in between titters, of the scandalous use of this behemoth in the center of their room.

"Mother," said Emma, suppressing a snicker. "I think I should like to give it a go."

"Emma! This ... implement is not for ladies of good breeding. And besides, you could catch a cold or worse, la grippe!"

"But mother, the lady said that she herself would bring up hot water for me to use with a bar of lavender soap. Oh please, mummy. I want to experience the full immersion into the culture of France. Surely they are not so scandalous!"

Anne looked askance at her daughter who seemed to be so gullible that she would believe that the body needed scrubbing. Perhaps the French ladies of leisure needed this but an English lady, as was well-known, was a self-cleaning entity, rather like a cat. She looked at her daughter who was excited about soaking in this French cesspool.

"Very well, Emma, but please be sure to acquire the appropriate attire for this soak."

"But mummy, one goes in as God intended us," said Emma with a glint in her eye.

"I beg your pardon?" she said, but almost before she had spoken, the full import had sunk in. "Well, I shall depart to the café and enjoy a glass of wine in the lady's parlor," declared Anne. "Nell, I hope you can help your mistress with her undress, but I will ask you to join me in the parlor downstairs thereafter."

"Yes, ma'am," said Nell. Just at that moment, Madame de Mortier, the hôteliere, entered with a selection of eaux de cologne and two maids carrying large buckets of steaming water. Emma jumped with glee, and clapped her hands. "Look mummy! It is so scandalous!"

Madame de Mortier looked at the two English ladies, the one, disapproving and the other filled with glee, and turned away with a frown, distributing the towels on the bath chair, and the various perfumes and soap around the tub. The two maids proceeded to empty the water into the tub with a flourish. Nell ignored the maids and without a word they departed, leaving Madame de Mortier to inform Emma about the method of performing one's ablutions.

Madame de Mortier closed the door behind her. Emma looked at the tub, steaming welcomingly, and grinned eagerly. "Nell," she said coyly. "Would you assist me in undressing?"

Nell looked at her with profound weariness. "I shall help you to unfasten your corset, my lady, but I am afraid I shan't remain while you *deshabille*. Allow me to help you with your frock coat." She helped Emma with the frock coat, and to unlace her corset and bodice. She also unlaced her high-topped shoes.

"I'm sorry Emma, but your mother says to leave you on your own," said Nell, as she ran after Emma's mother, who sailed out the door like a ship in full sail.

Emma was left to untie her shoes and remove her stockings. She used the chair to sit on, and trailed her fingers in the water that was scented with lavender. Then she unlaced her bodice and corset, and felt her body relax after the tension of the day.

She felt the warm air on her naked skin and relished the sensation. It was so strange and unfamiliar to her that she hardly knew what to do. She ran her fingers down her body, feeling the curves and turns. She then dropped the remainder of her clothing, moved to the bedpan that lay nearby and relieved herself. Then, with some hesitation, she gingerly stepped into the warm water of the bathtub. The sensation that washed over her body was stunning and wonderful.

Emma felt a tingling in her body that coursed through every vein and organ of her body. She lay back in the bath and reached for the lavender scented soap, rubbing it on her breasts and then over her arms. She was very surprised that her nipples rose to the occasion and she quickly began to massage them to allow them to return to their usual supple shape. Feeling this tingling in her nipples inspired her to wash her belly and crotch. She lifted her leg and ran the bar of soap all up and down.

Then she began to rub between her legs, in an effort to clean her nether regions. The sensation of this soft cloth was astonishing; she was suddenly very grateful that she was alone, for she was just a bit ashamed of her behavior. She gasped at the sensation, and lay back in the tub, letting the water wash over her, taking away the soapy bubbles that were accumulating in the hair of her nether regions.

Suddenly, this other-worldly experience became magical and she felt as though she were in a dream. The scent of beautiful lavender fields, the soft and warm water washing over her, cleansing her body, made her feel alive in a way she had never known possible. She began to rub the sides of her thighs with the slightly abrasive side of the cloth. She wondered what it was made of - muslin? Who knew? Although it was doing wonders for her; wonders she had never dreamt of before this day.

Her left hand was between her legs, gently rubbing on something that she could not identify. In truth, she did not know her body very well and this sensation was new to her, although the yearning was familiar. She placed her right hand on her chest, gently rubbing the firm nipple; it sent a sensation down her body, expanding the feeling of wonder. Little jolts were shooting down her legs and she spread them a little wider to allow her to gently rub the area between them, where the two folds meet. And then it suddenly became much easier to rub; a lubrication was now apparent from inside her body, protecting her from the sensation of rawness.

As Emma set the cloth over her stomach, warming herself, she inserted her finger into this area, noting that there were several sensitive areas that needed - or to which she wanted to give - attention. She had never known that this part of her body could be so sensitive. She put a finger gingerly inside her hole, noting the feelings of goodwill and happiness that coursed through her. And to add to the excitement, there was a small nub, a kind of skin-covered button that, when touched, gave her a feeling that so filled her with joy that she almost cried out.

In and out she moved, brushing the little button, until a feeling of goodwill washed over her, and her whole body relaxed in a way she had not felt since she was a child.

She lay in the water which had maintained much of its heat, until she regained her composure. Then she rose from the water, feeling the brisk air in the room that had cooled off since Nell left the fire in the grate to die down.

Reaching over to the chair, she took one of the amazingly fluffy towels and ensconced herself in its warmth. She quickly toweled off and began to dress in her second set of clothing. She was glad that she had taken the time to dry herself off, as her mother warned her of the grippe that could overtake her and kill her. But her body was tingling with excitement as her clothing began to cover her. It occurred to Emma that it was far more natural to remain uncovered. She resolved to try this again at her earliest opportunity.

Before she had completely dressed, Nell and her mother knocked on the door and to her "entrez!" she opened the wooden door to the bed chamber. Anne was surprised to see that Emma had dressed and resumed reading a novel.

"I see you've finished. Did it give you la grippe?" she asked.

Emma laughed. "Mother, it was a perfectly delightful experience. In fact, I hope very much to do it again!"

Nell turned away, seeing to her wardrobe. "Well, it smells quite pleasant," she said, sniffing quietly.

"It's lavender, Nell," said Emma. "It's lovely. One day I will make sure you soak in a lavender bath." Emma rang the bell to summon the French maids to empty the tub, whose water was now quite cold and becoming brackish from the soap scum and assorted pieces of detritus that had fallen from her body.

"It's a sight, though," said Anne. "How on earth does one rid oneself of all that rubbish?"

"The maids will be up presently," said Emma, as the door chimed and the two maids, laden with buckets, entered and began to drain the tub, clean it, and spritz the room with pleasantly flowery aromas.

"Merci beaucoup, mes demoiselles[2]," said Emma as the maids left with the buckets filled and the room sparkling clean and fresh again.

"Do you fancy a meal, maman?" asked Emma.

"I do wish you'd cease calling me maman; you make me feel like uncomfortably French," said Anne.

"Very well, Mother, I shall take note to preserve that title for your old age. Now, lets us go and seek some refreshment. There is a café in the main floor, is there not?"

"Indeed. I was just there, studying the menu. They have some peculiar items on offer, I must say. Not a crumpet to be seen."

"I am very eager to see what they have," said Emma, leading the way to the restaurant.

---

[2] Thank you very much, ladies.

The meal was a revelation for Emma because, similar to the bath, which seemed absurd at first, but ended by being a great joy, the meal, a delicious stew of chicken with potatoes, carrots, in a red wine and tarragon sauce. It was delightfully fragrant and quite unlike anything either of them could remember tasting before. The wine that accompanied the meal was something of a novelty to Emma as well. In England, young ladies rarely drank wine and this wine had a similar effect on her as the bath she had just experienced; her body flushed and her cheeks became somewhat inflamed, making her rather more enticing to the more daring gentlemen who frequented the ladies' lounge in the bistro. Noting these sidelong glances, Emma observed to her mother that gentlemen, it seems, prefer a young lady who looks as though she has taken some exercise. And since it was her first taste of really fine wine, rather than the sort of thing her father served, she drank rather more than she should have, finding herself a little unsteady on the climb to the room.

Once in bed though, Emma fell into a stupor, and did not wake until the morning. And when she awoke she found herself with a bit of a headache, cured rapidly by the café au lait served to them before they embarked on the journey to Paris aboard their *diligence*.

Chapter 3. Paris, City of Light

"Mother, have you been to Paris before?" asked Emma as they neared the capital.

"Of course," said Anne. "Why do you ask?"

"It is just that many of the landmarks I was prepared to encounter seem different from what I had expected."

"In what manner? It is true that the city has been through a war, and an occupation, but I am sure it is quite majestic."

"I suppose," said Emma with a frown. "I had read in the books of Fanny Burney about Notre Dame Cathedral, but I was absolutely unprepared for the glory that is the Champs-Élysées and the Arc de Triomphe, both of which seem brilliant!"

"Quite right," said Anne. "They are the height of modernity. It is remarkable that only two years ago, all the crowned heads of

Europe had marched here in victory after the defeat of Napoleon."

"Yes," said Emma, in wonder at each new sight that came through the diligence window. "It is so grand and peaceful, and all the French ladies are calm and well-dressed."

"And to think that a place that had been the site of so much misery such a short while ago could be transformed into the height of modernity so quickly. The resilience of the Gallic race is amazing," said Anne, as both she and Emma sat glued to the windows of the coach as they rumbled through the cobblestone streets.

"I confess that many of these shops are more beautiful, grander, and more imaginative than anything I had seen even in London."

"Really?" said Emma. "I had imagined that London was the height of fashion, given its size and its importance in the life of England," she said wistfully. She had never let her imagination run away with her to such an extent that she could possibly have imagined the wonder that was the Paris boutique.

"Mother," said Emma with a sense of wonder. "This is a beautiful street and I cannot even imagine anything so grand, even in London, but where are all the trees?"

"You know, darling, the occupying armies who encamped around this street only a few short years ago, used the stately trees of the Champs-Élysées as firewood. If you look carefully, you can see those little saplings that are trying to reach the sky. They are all that is left. I daresay in one hundred years, it will be a grand tree-lined avenue once again. I feel it gives the street a certain barrenness, don't you think?"

"I do indeed, Mother. It is melancholy to see such frivolity. But tell me, what is a "Bistro"? I have heard ever so many sorts of things but do not recall the term."

"Oh, my dear, it is quite droll, really. You see, the Russians occupied this city until a few years ago. They are brutes, you know, the Russians, and their soldiers were unable to sit still for a moment, even to shovel their borscht into their gullets. The French restaurants are notorious for slow and stately service, and so some of the smaller places began to advertise that they had rapid service to attract the Russians. 'Bistra' is the Russian word for 'quick' and so the restaurants that had fast service began to call themselves 'bistros'."

"Well in that case, since I have no desire to encounter a Russian brute and I do not want to shovel borscht into my gullet, let us avoid such establishments while we are here!"

"My dear, I do not think we shall be encountering any marauding Russian Hussars on the Champs-Élysées! I do believe they have long since returned to their wintery homes in Moscow."

"Well, thank the Lord for small mercies," said Emma. Then, seeing a number of grand hotels along the way, "Mother, do tell me where we shall be staying. For I am in grave need of a bath!"

"Oh Emma, do not even joke about such things. That bath you had is not to become a habit. It is one of those frightful things the Earl of Harewood was talking about: something to be avoided! For it smacks of decadence. And decadence is the beginning of the end."

"Oh mother," declared Emma. "You sometimes seem so provincial!"

"Remember, my dear daughter, that the European sensibilities are not ours, and if you intend to find an Englishman of good standing, these sorts of values will not stand you in good stead. Wild notions are distinctly disturbing for a well-bred Englishwoman, and you really must try to get them out of your head."

Emma sat back in the *diligence* and let the cobblestone streets lull her into a reverie. Before long, they pulled up in front of a small hotel called *Le Meurice* on the Rue Saint-Honoré which was not so grand as the other hotels but with a somewhat respectable façade.

"Is this where we must stay, mother?" asked Emma, as the carriage ground to a halt in the courtyard.

"I daresay, it is the finest hotel our modest means can afford. And this ruffian who is transporting us insists, unless my rudimentary French has failed me, that this is the place for an English traveler because they speak English here. That a blessing in this foreign place."

And as she spoke these words, a powerfully built Frenchman approached the carriage, and exchanged words with the coachman, Benoit. Anne opened the door and tried to instruct the man to carry their trunks to their room.

"My driver here tells me you let rooms to Englishmen."

The Frenchman, doffing his floppy cap, looked up at Anne, and smiled.

"Yes Madame, we offer rooms to ze English gentry. I trust you will be comfortable 'ere." He seemed pleased with his sentence, and Anne smiled recognizing his labors.

"It appears to be quite suitable. Have you chambers that would be proper for a lady and her daughter, of marriageable age?"

"Certainement, Mademoiselle[3]," he said, slipping back into his native tongue. Anne was taken aback by this slip. He clearly noted her discomfort and began to speak English again.

"I am certain zat madame and mademoiselle will be 'appy in our chambers."

"Capital!" said Anne. At this moment, Emma emerged from the carriage, and the man smiled broadly with what struck Anne as a lascivious leer. She frowned, and assumed a matronly demeanor. "Young man," she said in a condescending tone. "Do please remember your manners. Please go with my lady's maid and procure for us this suite of rooms and it would be ideal if it were on the main floor. We shall need two bed chambers

---

[3] Certainly, Miss.

and a drawing room. Have you such an apartment?"

"Oui madame," said the valet. "Please to following me, lady maid." Without correcting his execrable grammar, the two ladies were led to the grand lobby of the hotel. Brightly lit with gaslight, it was most impressive and Emma gasped with delight, smiling broadly. Anne nudged her and gave her a look that was as much as to say 'do not let them see that you are impressed.' Nevertheless, Emma was awestruck.

"But mother, it is simply delightful," she whispered. "Look at the gaslight! I have rarely seen anything so grand!"

"I know, my dear, but it is most indecorous to appear impressed."

Within the hour, they were in their chambers, on the second floor, with a grand view of the rue Saint-Honoré. This was a beautiful street, lined with cafés and hotels, teeming with grand Parisian foot traffic.

Emma stared out the window, desperate to join the crowd.

"Oh mother, can we venture out to discover the sights? I am simply dying to walk."

Anne looked exhausted. "I really must take a moment, darling," she said. "But I am told a young lady can walk by herself with only a maid as companion in Paris, so long as she stays to the main arteries. I should let you discover the city if you are in need of excitement, Emma."

Emma was astonished, excited, and a trifle frightened. "Oh yes, mother!" she said. "I shall go to the lobby again and inquire as to the sights I should see. I shall be gone for only a few hours, I assure you. Thank you, mother!" she said, motioning for Nell to follow.

In the street, Emma maintained her composure. In point of fact, it was scandalous even for a Parisian lady to go unaccompanied in the streets, but never caring for the niceties of social convention, Emma sailed down the avenue with aplomb.

"Nell," she said with authority. "You must walk ahead of me or behind me." When Nell looked at her, hurt, she added. "Keep abreast me but do not look as though you were with me. I adore scandalizing the locals!"

Nell was well used to this silliness, shook her head without so much as a word, and stepped ahead, knowing that Emma would dawdle.

On the way, Emma looked into some of the finer shops, selling mainly beautiful trinkets and baubles. Some jewelry shops displayed marvelous necklaces, brooches, and rings, making Emma wish she had a beau who would shower her with these sorts of things. Truth be told, she was scarcely interested at all in jewels and other trivialities; her interest was in dresses. But she confessed that she was very taken with the beauty of some of these items.

"Nell," she said sharply. "Do come and give me your advice about these little trinkets."

"Yes, milady," said Nell. "However, I could never give you advice about these things. I was never brought up to appreciate anything as grand as this."

"Of course not, but do you think I should adorn myself with these baubles?"

"You milady? Why of course! You'd look right grand with them on your'n."

Emma had condescended to talk to Nell as an equal, but as soon as she betrayed her common roots, she lost this desire. "Very well, Nell. You can be on your way." And Nell obeyed, stepping ahead so as not to draw attention.

Emma moved from shop to shop until she reached the Champs-Élysées. Here, the road was much broader and the crowds were more boisterous. She strode along the avenue, looking in the windows, until she was stopped by her amazement in front of a little dress shop called *Au Petit Dunkerque*, which displayed a dress that was so beautiful that she could restrain herself no longer. She had behaved with great dignity and reserve for nearly an hour, she felt, but this shop had a dress so beautiful that it eclipsed everything she had seen up to that point. It was the very dress that she imagined, her suitor would present to her as a token of his esteem on that fateful day when she would get engaged. It seemed to be made of spun gold; it was entrancing, the most beautiful gown she had ever seen. The Empire waist was of the most perfect cut, and the puffed sleeves gave it an elegance, a regal quality that was unlike anything she could have even imagined. The dress flared slightly in an elegant cone-shape that would have been the talk of society in London. It was embroidered with the most beautiful gilded leaves. The daring scoop-neck would reveal her ample bosom in a most attractive way. She decided to enter the shop.

Emma stepped into the small shop, and was greeted by a little Frenchman with a balding head and small wire-framed glasses.

His pug nose was turned up as though he were examining her. His blue velvet frock coat was splattered with what seemed to be some sort of soup.

"Bonjour mademoiselle," said the little man. "Je m'appelle Charles-Raymond Granchez, et je suis propriétaire de ce magasin.⁴"

"Enchantée," said Emma, in what she imagined was a far too English accent.

He immediately switched to English. "I see you come from England," said the little man.

"Indeed, I do and I must tell you, Monsieur Granchez, that frock you have in your window is the most beautiful thing I have seen in my life. What is it made of, pray?"

"Ah! Mademoiselle has an exquisite taste. It is made of sarcenet, a kind of silk zat is very light and comfortable. You can see ze renaissance style in ze sleeves. It is unique

---

[4] Good day, miss. My name is Charles-Raymond Granchez and I am the proprietor of this shop.

and I believe, mademoiselle, that you would be ze perfect owner of zeese little dress. Would you care to try it on?"

Emma was taken aback. Nell had not yet entered, and Emma suddenly felt it was inappropriate to be in the shop alone, unescorted. The idea that she would try on a dress in front of this little man was shocking to her. This thought was clearly displayed on her face, and Monsieur Granchez stepped back in defense. "I have a dressing chamber, of course, mademoiselle. And a lady's maid to 'elp you. Please, I have no interest in shock." He laughed.

These words served to placate her. "Very well," she said. "But my mother will have to give her permission for this purchase to go forward. I want to be clear. I carry no money with me."

"Mais oui, mademoiselle," said Granchez, adding, "Cosette! Viens ici tout de suite!" A beautiful, coquettish maid appeared from a back room. She was petite, and dressed in a magnificent gown that must have been of Granchez's creation. Her figure was trim and attractive and she had a stunningly beautiful face surrounded by delightful honey-blonde ringlets that made her seem wild and exquisitely sophisticated at the same time. Her smile was accentuated by the most perfect pearl-white teeth, in a mouth with full red lips that made her seem to be begging for a kiss. Emma felt a jolt in her body that she was at pains to identify. It was new and it was peculiar, but she knew at once that she would be having a great deal of fun with this young woman.

"Allo!" said Cosette. "I speak English for your convenience. Please miss, to step this way." And she made a grand gesture that indicated for Emma to step into the room behind the shop. At that moment, Nell entered the shop, and Monsieur Granchez looked at her, sized her up, and concluded immediately that she must be Emma's lady's maid. Emma herself looked at Nell, somewhat unhappily, and gestured for her to follow as she went through the door, as Cosette took the dress from the window.

In the small room, lit attractively with a beautiful chandelier, Emma took a seat on a divan in the center of the room, surrounded by mirrors. Nell took her place on the little stool at the foot of the divan. On the small table, there was a bottle of wine and a pair of small crystal wine glasses. Nell poured a small amount into one of the glasses as Cosette appeared with the dress. "Please help yourself to ze wine," she said, pouring a small glass for herself.

Cosette stopped, stepped back, admiring Emma's figure in her dress that at one time had seemed very fashionable, but suddenly seemed terribly pedestrian. All of a sudden Emma felt shy.

"Let's get that thing off you," said Cosette with a change of mood. "What is your maid's name please?"

"This is Nell," said Emma with a grand gesture.

"Nell, can you please help me to dress your mistress? I must make her look as beautiful as I know she is." She reached to take Emma's hands to help her up, while tossing the beautiful golden dress to Nell, who deftly caught it with one hand. Cosette began untying Emma at the back and gently easing the dress down her body. Emma, unaccustomed to the touch of another on her body, began to feel tingling sensations, partly because of the wine, and partly because of the gentle and soothing ministrations of this beautiful lady's maid.

"Ah Cosette, I can do this myself," protested Emma, looking to Nell for help.

"I have it, miss," said Nell. "It is my job."

"You must forgive me," Cosette replied. "Permit me to introduce myself. I am Cosette de Francoeur. I am nineteen years of age, and I want very much to be a couturière. I am not a maid; I am a woman who is preparing her own business. And you are?"

"My name is Emma Shaftesbury," she said. "I am twenty years old, from Canterbury, in England, and my mother and I are taking the Grand Tour. This is our first stop. This, of course, is Nell, my maid."

"Enchantée," said Cosette, looking superciliously at Nell. "How exciting that you are able to make ze Grand Tour!" and she really seemed to mean it. Without a word, she set to work taking off Emma's dress, with the aid of Nell. She worked with great speed and tenderness, massaging the small blemishes on Emma's body that were caused by the rubbing of material on her skin. Cosette admired Emma's alabaster complexion, unique among the strawberry blonde race, and gently touched her as each part of her body was revealed. In short order, she stood before Cosette, only her shift and her boots remained on.

Cosette, in a manner that was absolutely foreign and un-English, looked admiringly at Emma's form, and exclaimed, "But you have a beautiful figure, Miss Emma.

We need only accentuate what God gave you." And she began to minister to Emma with a tender hand. She ran her hand from Emma's neck, and down her bosom, to her slightly rounded stomach. "Do you see, Nell?" she said, making Nell blush to look at her mistress. Emma, stunned, did nothing to stop her, but enjoyed the feeling of intimacy.

Taking yet another glass of wine, Emma leaned back on the divan as Cosette lifted the beautiful golden dress with great ceremony over her head, and indicated for Nell to help her. Nell, finding some joy in this theatrical activity, took the other end of the dress, and carefully, with great love and tenderness, placed the dress over Emma's head. It slid easily down her body, and Emma moaned in satisfaction.

"It feels even more heavenly than it looks," she said, her eyes slightly closed, as though in ecstasy. With Nell's help, Cosette tied it securely behind her and moved behind the full-length mirror to show Emma the quality of the workmanship.

"What do you think?" she asked.

A visibly and audibly tipsy, Emma responded with enthusiasm. "Oh my Lord. I am stunning! Everyone will want to kiss me in this dress. Come, kiss me," she said to Cosette, who smiled and laughed, pretending not to understand.

"And so, should I wrap this gown up for you, mademoiselle?" she said.

"How much does it cost?" asked Emma.

"It is only twenty thousand and four hundred francs," said Cosette with a gesture indicating it was a pittance. Emma, who was unaccustomed to converting money in her head, looked confused. The wine had gone to her head and she was afraid she had done things that were inappropriate. She blushed. "Uh, yes, miss, Cosette. May I apologize for my behavior? I am unaccustomed to drinking wine, and I have just undertaken a long and arduous journey from Amiens. I hope I have not offended you."

Cosette smiled. "You have not," she said. Then she moved to Emma, taking her hand and straightening her skirts. "This is entirely within your rights, as a client in our dress shop." She was unaware that Cosette was unfastening the dress with great speed and before she knew it, she was once again standing in her shift with the dress at her feet. Cosette took the other dress from Nell and gently replaced it on Emma, who looked slightly dejected at the old dress that seemed so dull in comparison. At that moment, Monsieur Granchez entered the room, and smiled.

"Ah oui, mademoiselle. I see you are enjoying the wine."

Emma looked up, and smiled. "It is of excellent vintage," she remarked.

Monsieur Granchez took the golden gown that had given Emma such joy, and as he let his eyes linger on her shapely body, he bowed ceremoniously. "Shall I wrap the frock for you, Mademoiselle Emma?" he said.

"I beg you, sir," she said, in bewilderment. "Allow us a moment to finish our custom." Nell motioned to Monsieur

Granchez to leave, and he was suddenly mortified, realizing that a most inappropriate moment had passed between them. "Forgive me, I was not paying attention." He backed up through the door, with great ceremony, as Cosette continued to prepare the dress for packaging. Cosette, seeing that the effect of the wine was wearing off, helped her with alacrity, making sure all the ties and bonds were securely tied, and that Emma was modestly dressed.

"I must hasten to my mother," said Emma. "You said it was twenty thousand and four hundred livres?"

"We call them francs here now," said Cosette. "But I must ask my master." She exited through the small door and could be heard speaking in rapid-fire French.

"Do you love it, Nell?" asked Emma, still slightly inebriated.

"I do mistress, but it is so dear!"

"Indeed. That is a bother. I must ask mother if she will be able to spare a little for it."

"I mean, it is impossible Emma," said Nell, almost angrily. "It costs a fortune!"

In the next room, Monsieur Granchez appeared to be annoyed with Cosette, upbraiding her in a dialect that was so rapid that it was impossible to know its meaning. However, when he finished, he turned to Emma. "In view of the embarrassment that I caused, mademoiselle, I am prepared to offer this beautiful dress to you for only twenty thousand francs."

"I shall return," said Emma, swishing across the room to the door, and opening it rapidly, allowing herself into the street, as the two astonished shopkeepers looked on.

"Oh, mother, it is the most beautiful gown I have ever seen. Nell, tell her."

"It is indeed a very comely frock, ma'am," said Nell.

"Nay, it is the most beautiful gown anyone has ever seen," said Emma.

"Emma, have you been drinking?" said her mother.

"I had only a wip of sine in the shop," she said, dismissing the criticism.

"Well, I would be only too happy to see you in a new gown. Did you see how much it cost?" asked the woman who was born to shopkeepers.

"Twenty thousand and four hundred francs," said Emma, noting, "but they reduced it to twenty thousand for me because of a mishap."

Before she could gauge if her mother was approving or disapproving, and before she felt the need to explain what - precisely - this mishap was, her mother swooned to the chaise longue that was nearest them. Alarmed, Nell ran to the traveling chest to fetch the smelling salts. Emma stood before her collapsed mother, not knowing what to do. "Oh my dear mother, you must have caught a cold while you were sitting by the window!"

"Dear God, no!" said Nell, over the recumbent figure of her mother. "It's just that - do you not realize how much that would be in guineas?"

"Of course I don't!" snapped Emma, offended that Nell would treat her like a bourgeois commoner. And her own lady's maid, yet!

Nell administered the smelling salts to rouse Anne.

"Thank you, Nell," said Anne, turning to Emma. "Darling, I want to put this in some context for you, if I may. One pound is enough money to buy a sheep. Five hundred pounds is what it takes to raise a young woman of your station. Now, how much is a franc in English money? Well, it is difficult to say, but let us say that to convert this dress, which you say is made of spun gold, into money that we know in England, it would be more than enough to support you, your sister, and your brother for the rest of your natural lives, I warrant."

Emma heard this with horror. She had never considered that money had any particular use other than to buy things they needed, and the relative value of currencies was not a consideration of hers. Clearly, she could not get this dress.

"I understand, mother, and I'm sorry for being such a fool. I shall never ask you again for such a dear item. It is entirely my ignorance."

"I am curious though, my darling, about this beautiful dress. Do you think you could show it me?"

"Of course," said Emma sadly. "Come with me." She sadly walked up the Rue St. Honoré to the Champs-Élysées, to the little shop called *Au Petit Dunkerque*. As they approached it, she motioned to her mother to look in the window. There it was, as beautiful as ever, and her mother gasped, just as Emma had gasped when she saw it.

"My heavens, Emma," said Anne. "It is indeed the most beautiful frock I have ever laid eyes on. But my dear, you must understand that your father, as well-to do as he is, could never allow such a purchase. We have good English dressmakers who can make your dresses." She looked at the crestfallen young woman, and regretted ever having let her see such a dress. "I am so terribly sorry to have to deny you this beautiful dress, Emma, but I assure you there would be no place you could wear such a dress, other than your wedding day."

Emma knew her mother was right and, as headstrong as she could be in certain instances, she felt for her mother and understood the difficulty in allowing such an exorbitant purchase. She smiled. "You are a darling for indulging me, maman," said Emma. Turning to Nell, she said, with a twinkle in her eye. "Nell, you are a fast hand with a needle. Do you think you could make my dress a trifle comelier with a few French baubles?"

Nell, as always eager to please if it meant using her God-given talents, smiled and opened her eyes wide. "Miss Emma, I would be delighted to do such a task for ye."

"In that case, mother, what say we enter the shop and purchase some of the adornments that made that dress the perfect gown. Nell is very talented at dressmaking and I believe, with my encouragement and guidance, she could make this sow's ear into a silk purse." She was beaming, and Anne looked at her daughter with love and gratefulness.

"My daughter, you are the most intelligent young woman I know." Together they opened the door and entered the shop.

Chapter 4. Transalpine Trek

The following week, the two ladies and the overworked but diligent maid set off to their next destination on the Grand Tour: Venice. It is true it would take more than a week to journey first to Lyon, and from thence to Grenoble, across the Alps to Turin, feeling every bit like Hannibal atop an elephant. This journey was uneventful in their memories, despite the stunning beauty out the window of the coach. By this time, it was April, and rains had begun to lash the carriage windows.

Benoit, having returned to Calais much the richer, arranged for a world traveler with a more comfortable *diligence* coach to take them to Lyon, and suggested that perhaps the lady's maid should travel inside the coach, much to the gratitude of Nell, who had clung to the rails atop their carriage like a shipwrecked sailor from Calais to Paris.

Although travel was arduous and somewhat bumpy, mother and daughter took the time necessary to see what could be seen. "Do look out the window my dear; you never know the next time you will see these sights," said Anne to her daughter, who otherwise spent much of her time reading her novel. Emma had purchased an English copy of Fanny Burney's fantastical book called *The Wanderer*. "It is a most interesting book," said Emma to her mother. "I feel as though I were living through the Terror. And yet I cannot put it down!"

"Do look out the window and see the wonder that is France," said Anne, hoping to coax her daughter to lift her nose from the book.

"Yes mother," said Emma with a certain hesitation, not wanting to lose the thread of the story in her romance. For, in this compact little world, her heroine, with whom she related closely, was meeting dashing and mustachioed villains and cads, and rebuffing them with splendid quips. Emma saw herself as a heroine in some ways, and her letters home to her sister Elizabeth were filled with adventurous tales of her exploits, embellished by the active imagination of the young traveler.

"Dear Lizzie," she wrote. "Today we departed Lyon, which is a great deal like Paris. We visited Montmartre in Paris, where the wild artistes dwell, on the hill near the Roman church called Sacré Cœur. I had a most pleasant encounter with a painter who desired to paint my portrait. Of course I rebuffed him, and was adamant that I should not be the subject of a painting, but I confess to feeling flattered ever so much.

"Lyon has a similar hilly terrain, and like Paris, it has those charming bridges across its river, called the Rhône. We enjoyed the beautiful dress shops in Lyon, but nothing could compare to the dress at *Au Petit Dunkerque* in Paris. Oh Lizzie, you would be so charmed by the French! They are a delight in every way. I am frightened to cross into Italy, as I speak very little of their language. Mama insists one need not converse with the locals to absorb the charms of the place, and I trust her judgment implicitly. Do give my love to daddy and Sebastian. Yours ever faithfully, Emma."

And time passed, Emma learned more and more, and Anne learned more and more about Emma. Nell had successfully adorned Emma's simple dress to give it a continental flair, that made her feel very sophisticated. They had purchased some beautiful silk adornments to make the dress seem fashionable again, and Emma was very happy looking as charming as she did. She was quite certain that several of the gentlemen with whom she was sharing the compartment of the *diligence* had looked admiringly at her dress, although she did not dare to engage them in conversation.

And they stayed for a few days in Lyon, to rest and secure transport across the Alps. This proved more difficult to do as the private coachmen were never fond of crossing borders to other lands. They managed to secure passage on a public conveyance though, and boarded this public coach. The three of them (Nell travelling as though she too were a lady of standing) set off across the Alps, bound for Turin.

The journey across the Alps was arduous and uncomfortable, cold and unforgiving. Anne was stoic in the face of challenges like these, as she was born to a family used to difficulties, whereas Emma, having lived a life of relative comfort, was shocked by the bitter winds that blew through the windows of the bumpy carriage.

At one point, an axle on the *diligence* broke and they were forced to stand in the cold while the coachman fixed it, which took more than an hour, and despite the beauty of Emma's dress, it was ineffectual against the blistering cold surrounding her. Nevertheless, her mother's good humor and Nell's patience convinced her to be somewhat more reasonable about her discomfort.

"Mother," she said, while blowing on her frozen fingers. "This was not something I ever dreamt I would have to endure, but I am glad for the experience. It is difficult and bone-chilling, but I wouldn't trade it for anything. I shall have tales to tell before this journey is done, I warrant."

"Indeed you shall, milady," said a gentleman standing by her clad in a huge great coat. "I may offer you the shelter of my coat if you are amenable to the offer of a kindly stranger."

At first, Emma ignored this effrontery while she could, but at a point when she felt she might die of exposure, she turned to the travelling Englishman, and smiled. "I would be most grateful for your kindness sir," she said. "If I may have the coat, I would probably owe you my life."

The kindly gentleman took off his great coat and wrapped her in it, giving her a warm and inviting respite from the cold.

"I thank you for your kindness, sir," she said. "Perhaps I should know the identity of my guardian angel."

"Sir Percy Fothergill, esquire, milady," he said, with some degree of ceremony. "I am embarking on the Grand Tour, as ordered by my father. Having finished at Eton and before I get entirely lost at Oxford, he decided, in his ultimate wisdom that I should freeze to death somewhere between heaven and hell. I suppose this is as good a place to die as any," he quipped, smiling at her. "And whom do I have the pleasure of addressing?" he asked.

"Oh, my stars, you are correct, Mr. Fothergill," said Emma, looking at her mother, who seemed to give her blessing for this indiscretion. "I confess I have never spoken to a man to whom I have not been introduced," she said, "and so I beg your indulgence. My name is Lady Emma Shaftesbury, from Kent. My mother and I are making the Grand Tour as well, and like you, I feared for my life until you offered your great coat. I am deeply grateful for your kindness."

"'Tis nothing," he said, crossing his arms, although Emma could see that he was very cold. She, snug in her warmth, smiled at him and, sensing the lag in conversation, dug in her mind for things to talk about.

"I see you will be going to Oxford. That must be a very exciting proposition," she said.

Percy Fothergill smiled. "I daresay it will be a challenge, for a lad as dull as I. I was as poor a student at Eton as it was possible to be, and yet somehow, I was admitted to Oxford, on condition that I not take any class that would be even slightly interesting."

Emma smiled at his modesty, noting that he was well-built and well-spoken. "In view of your innate dullness, I trust your father planned your trip wisely. Will you be seeing the antiquities?"

"If you mean, did my father ensure that I only see only people he knows, then aye, that was his plan. I am indebted to you for foiling it. For I am quite sure that he did not foresee my meeting such a pretty young lady here on this godforsaken mountainside."

"We are bound for Venice, you see. My mother, yonder, is my guardian. Who, pray tell, is yours?"

"Why, it's my father, the gentleman who has doffed his great coat for your mother. My valet is the lad who has offered his cloth coat to your maid. It seems we are all well met. And I would wager that he has eyes only for your mother, and will not see anything we do," said the cad.

Emma, scandalized by his kind of talk, would have blushed if she had not already been red in the face. Indeed, her fingers, blue with the cold, were the only part of her that had not gone the color of her hair. Mr. Fothergill seemed to have been taken with her curious hair color and smiled as he raised his eyes to her once again. "Miss Shaftesbury, I am very taken with your red tresses. Is there a little Celtic in your roots?"

Emma knew not how to respond, for she was unaccustomed to these sorts of personal remarks. She was, though, more than able to fend for herself and she turned to him with an air of sauciness. "My dear sir, I am not sure why you think that lending an article of apparel is cause for excessive familiarity. Please refrain from this behavior in future. I was speaking of the glories of Venice, and you can seem to talk of nothing but my personal appearance. Pray tell me what you have seen so far on your journey."

Taken aback, Sir Percy was ashamed and humbled. He knit his brow and doffed his top hat. "I beg forgiveness, Miss Shaftesbury. I meant no offense. I was merely noting that it is rare to meet a young lady with such a beauteous head of hair. It is worthy of mention, I would wager."

"If you would wager that, my dear fellow, you would lose. And I am well enough aware of the cads in the world who think nothing of ruining a young lady's reputation with such effrontery. Good day!" With that, she tossed his great coat into the snow, striding away to where her mother stood. She was talking with the father of the young man who had proved so unworthy. *Truly, she thought to herself, this young man must have been quite the dullest student in the entire school, if he had indeed attended Eton.* She approached her mother who was, like herself, taken by surprise by the effrontery of the young man's father.

"Mother," said Emma, as she got within hearing distance. "I wish to re-enter the carriage. Will you join me?"

Her mother looked and noted that the driver was finished with his work and the carriage was once again serviceable. "I shall be glad to join you my dear," she said, sailing past the older man, who looked crestfallen.

"This gentleman was most forward," she added. "I wonder about the people one meets in foreign lands, having lost their sense of decorum. Do you know he invited me to the masked ball in Venice? I had to inform him that I was both a married woman and a mother, and that his invitation was unwelcome and unseemly."

But Emma could also see that her mother was somewhat flattered at the attention of this rather attractive gentleman. "Oh mother," said Emma. "I agree, but I must say that to have the attention of a gentleman of good standing whilst in the frigid air was somewhat diverting. And I was able to stay quite warm in that young man's great coat. Sadly, it will be of scant use to him now that it is coated with ice."

"Oh Emma, that was unkind."

"Perhaps, mother, but I have little sympathy for a cad, regardless of his age. You know, mother, I do believe I have spent all my capital on my search for an Englishman to wed. Perhaps I should look for a husband among the Italians I encounter."

"My dear, that is a mad idea! Do you not know how difficult it is to find a suitable fit for you even among your own race? To then consider a foreigner as a suitor is sheer folly," said Anne to her daughter, not knowing if she were serious. "In any case, we must re-enter this woebegone carriage before we both catch our deaths. Did you see our Nell?"

The two ladies looked around and saw Nell sporting the cloth coat of the valet, and they gestured wildly for her to rejoin them in the carriage. When Nell spied them, she appeared to consider the possibility of running away and leaving their employ forever, but came swiftly to her senses and rejoined the ladies in the carriage, followed by the valet, who seemed frightened by the two ladies. Nonetheless, he realized he had no choice but to re-enter, having lost his protection from the elements to Nell.

The carriage got moving again within a few minutes, and the cold seemed to dissipate as they crossed the mountain pass, and started on toward Turin.

"Mother, is there anything undying to be seen at Turin?" asked Emma.

"There is the legendary shroud of Turin. It is said to have the impression of Christ on it."

"The impression? Whatever do you mean? I've never heard of such a thing."

"It is one of the wonders of the world and the only impression we have of the Christ. No other image exists that shows what he actually looked like."

"I suppose I should see that, although it is hardly a great work of art, is it?"

"I suppose not, but they have an Egyptian museum in Turin, where we can see artefacts from the cradle of civilization."

Emma yawned, and rolled her eyes. "Is there any way to eat at a restaurant, and continue to Venice? I hear there is a masked ball in the Piazza filled with noblemen from the old Venetian families."

Anne sighed and then smiled to herself; it appeared as though Emma would not be very inspired by the great art of the ancient world. Her daughter - to her relief - was more interested in courting than art galleries!

Lisa Brooks

Chapter 5. Touring Turin and Venetian Adventures

The shroud of Turin was every bit as scintillating as they had expected. If there had been something that was less interesting, neither Anne nor Emma could think of it. It did lead them to a great inspiration though - the inspiration that they should leave Turin as soon as possible. Their flight was only briefly halted when they realized that they needed to sample the new establishment called the "Ristorante." Although they had been familiar with public houses and meals in inns and hotels since they left Dover, the ristorante was something new.

Anne and Emma made arrangements through the locandiere at the inn to attend this establishment called *Scaramuccia*, which was a beautifully appointed drawing room in a fine building, with a large number of tables illuminated by candlelight at each and a spray of chandeliers above them, with hundreds, perhaps thousands of white tapers. The beauty of the room was awe-inspiring, and the beautifully calligraphed card listing the dishes to be served, called the *prezzo fisso*, listed an *aperitivo* which was a plate of ripe black olives, something Emma had never before tastes, and to which she would be forever devoted thereafter. The next dish was called an *antipasto* which featured local sausages that had been finely shaved into tiny slices. Their salty deliciousness was accompanied by a stale bread called a *crostino*. While Emma enthused about the delight of such exotic food, Anne was thoroughly confused, not having seen any roasted meat at all.

Thereafter, there appeared on the table something called a *bagna caoda*, which seemed to be a thick sauce into which one dipped vegetables that had not been sufficiently boiled. Then a young man brought them a dish he called pesto which had elaborately shaped pieces of unleavened bread, boiled and dipped in a wonderful sauce made out of basil and garlic, and dusted with an excellent hard cheese.

"Mother, I do believe these Piedmontese have created an art out of eating; I haven't been able to identify a single thing yet!" she enthused.

Her mother was not as convinced. "I have heard the most frightful things about this spice they call garlic," she said. "They say it wards off evil spirits, but I wonder if it is not responsible for just as many evil spirits in itself."

"Mother! I am shocked!" said Emma. "But to be frank, I am curious what sort of sweet they will serve as dessert." And as she said this, a young liveried servant deposited a strange dish on the table before them, and distributed two plates. "What is this?" ventured Emma.

"Che?" said the young man, clearly not understanding.

"Mother, do you know any of this tongue? This Italian?"

"Quella tipo de dolce è[5]?" said Anne, wowing her daughter with her linguistic abilities.

"È una Mostarda di frutta, madamina[6]," he said, proudly. "Se non lo vuoi, abbiamo anche una torta di nocciola[7]," he said.

"No, è perfetto, grazie[8]," she said proudly smiling.

"Dear God, mother! You astound me," said Emma. It is indeed one of those truths that one observes within the family that the child presumes the parent sprang fully formed from the head of Zeus the moment they themselves were born, and hence they are astonished when the parent displays knowledge that predates their birth.

"You know, when I was a young girl, my mother took me on a tour of Italy, and I had the good fortune to be able to engage a tutor,

---

[5] What sort of dessert is this?

[6] It's a Mostarda with candied fruit, milady.

[7] If you do not want it, we also have a hazelnut cake.

[8] No, this is perfect.

who taught be the fundamentals of Italian. So do not be so surprised, my dear, that I have some knowledge that you did not know about. Now let us sample the Piedmontese delicacy before us." And with that, Anne dug her spoon into the fruit.

Emma beat her to it though and her reaction was swift and definitive. "Oh mother, it is vile!" she said, rather too loud for the restaurant to ignore. Heads turned and smiled, knowingly. Anne looked at her daughter askance, as she tasted the *Mostardo*, and the moment it hit her mouth she was likewise nauseated.

"Emma, you must not speak so," she said. And then she added, under her breath. "It truly is the vilest thing I have ever put in my mouth." She gesticulated at the smiling waiter, who approached them with two plates already laden with the hazelnut cake.

"È come avevo temuto," he said. "Per favore, permettimi di presentarti la torta alla nocciola!9"

"Oh mummy, tell me we don't have to suffer any longer!" said Emma with a frown.

"This is a proper dessert, Emma," said Anne, nodding to the waiter.

They both dug their forks into the cake and felt a sudden relief.

"Mummy," said Emma, reverting to her childish self. "I am praying that we do not have any more surprises with the food in this land."

"I will make every effort to save you from alien food, my daughter," said Anne, smiling. She had no desire to tell her daughter that this *Mostarda* had been her idea; that she was testing the boundaries of her daughter's interest in the foreign. Fortunately though, she came to realize that things were not as far gone as she had feared.

---

[9] It is as I had feared. Please, permit me to present you with the hazelnut cake.

Chapter 6. Venice

"Although things are far from normal, and everything is different from what I remember of England, I confess I am having the time of my life," Emma wrote to her sister Elizabeth from the hotel in Venice. She neglected to mention the atrocious dessert she'd had in Turin, nor did she mention the arduous journey from Turin in an Italian coach that seemed to have been sprung with swords, as her mother had said. The journey was made better by the delightful weather once they had passed the Alps, and the sun shining on them in the way that only northern Italian suns do was cheering to the pair as they made their way, amid the incomprehensible babble of Italian travelers.

Emma was once or twice accosted in a most disturbing way by one or two gentlemen who wanted to make her acquaintance. "And," her mother reminded her, "although these Italians have different ways of making themselves known to a lady, *we* are English women and as such we must maintain our rigorous standards. We must not speak to men who have not been introduced to us. Especially if they speak no English, and particularly if they are older than what we consider to be marriageable age."

"Odd," she remarked to her sister. "The elderly or middle-aged Italian gentleman seems not to have invested in a looking glass; or, if he has, it must be one of those satirical looking glasses that Jonathan Swift mentioned, wherein one sees everyone's reflection but one's own!"

As she penned this witticism, she felt very grown up and witty. "But also," she remarked, "these gentlemen seem not to have noticed that their wisps of grey are not the sort of spun gold this lady had in mind for her trousseau."

At her writing table overlooking the Grand Canal just north of the Rialto Bridge, she felt very much the world traveler. "Lizzie darling," she wrote. "You must know that this is the loveliest little town in the world.

And today, we have a special event that has been organized by a gentleman who has taken us under his wing here, at the Serenissima Hotel. It is a recreation of the Carnival events the local gentry indulge in once a year. Of course, it is far too late in the season to do anything like what they did (which would frighten me to death of course), but let me explain what lies in store for me and mamma.

"At dusk, we have been asked to don a mask and a costume depicting one of these comic characters. They have a series of characters from their theater they call Commedia dell'arte, which is essentially an Italian Punch and Judy show. I shall be Colombina, and mamma will be la Signora. It will be such fun! As I understand it, we will all be wearing some sort of costume and we shall even interact with the local gentry in a wonderful festive dance. Indeed, we had a seamstress in the chambers fitting me and mamma (for I have taken to calling her that) for these wonderful costumes. I shall report on the result."

"Emma! Do come and allow Nell to dress you!" called Anne to her daughter who was furiously scribbling letters.
"I shall be there in a moment, mamma," she called.
"Shall I accompany the two of you to this event, my lady?" said Nell, looking bored. She had not been having a good time in Venice, owing to her inability to speak the language.
"I do not think so, Nell. You should take some time to yourself."
Emma burst into the room at that moment. "Well, strip me and truss me up!" she said, giggling. Nell, without a word, proceeded to dress Emma in the very flattering costume.
"This costume I am wearing... other than being jolly revealing, what is it supposed to be?"

"They call it Columbina, the inamorata," said her mother.

"And just who is this inamorata?" asked Emma.

"My lady, she is the one all the young men fall in love with?"

"That sounds fun, although I don't doubt they would with all this skin visible."

"Come, come, Emma, it shows no more skin than many of your ball gowns."

"Yes I suppose you are right," she said, twirling in front of the looking glass.

They tell me it is an eighteenth-century style," she said, looking at the beautiful red velvet over-jacket that she wore over a beautiful flowing gown of green satin.

"It is beautiful and very flattering to your slim waist," said Anne, comparing her rather frumpy outfit, making her look distinctly unattractive, as the 'matron." Emma wore red high-heeled boots that gave her several inches of height so that she towered over her mother Anne, and the décolleté of her collar was risqué in the extreme. The more Anne looked at Emma as she twirled in front of the mirror, clearly feeling pretty, alluring, and daring, the more uncomfortable she became.

"Perhaps we should call off this affair" said Anne.

"What? Whatever for, mamma?"

"Emma I am having second thoughts, I confess," she said.

But Emma would not be put off. "Oh mother," she said pleadingly. "This shall be the biggest excitement of my young life. Do not forbid me! And mamma," she added. "What were all those lessons for if not to show my abilities as a dancer? I was always the best in England and I would love to show these Italians how it is done!"

"Very well!" said Anne, realizing that her daughter was far more mature than she had given her credit for. "We may go. Now: where did they say to meet?"

"We must be in the lobby precisely at six," she said, glancing at the clock on the mantle. It read five minutes to six. "I wonder, though, mamma, do you think they are punctual here? After all, it is a different sort of city from the rest of Italy."

"In my experience, that is not one of their weaknesses," she said smiling. She opened the door to their room, and slid the key which was hung on a silver chain around her neck, down her cleavage, feeling naughty.

In the lobby, several of the English guests had congregated already, and were walking to and fro, showing off their frocks, and their costumes. There were several young men, who looked quite dandyish in the Arlecchino outfits, and two other Colombina costumes.

"Mamma," said Emma. "I believe I am truly lucky. I believe my costume is the finest of them all."

"Indeed it is," said Anne with a certain air of chagrin.

Emma went ahead of her mother, to join the group of young people, barely noticing the older people, dressed more creatively and more interestingly.

Anne shook her head and turned to one of the ladies standing with her. "It is a curious thing about the young: they appear to turn their elders to stone when it comes to society. It is not a matter of disrespect - it is simply that they do not credit them as existing at all!"

"Indeed!" said the older lady. "I have not spoken to my daughter in hours!"

Suddenly Anne felt fortunate to have such a lovely young woman for her daughter.

The tour leader, a young Italian nobleman named Fabio appeared shortly, nearly exactly on time, impressing Anne with his punctuality. He also impressed Emma with his fine legs, prominently displayed to the scandal of the young English ladies.

"Signore e signorine," he said grandly. "I am most happy to invite you to the most Venetian festival of them all. We have a beautiful string orchestra to play for you and dances that will enchant you. Please come with me to the fleet of gondole I have prepared, and we shall go to the grandest drawing room in Europe, the Piazza San Marco!"

There was a cooing among the youthful English crowd - seven of them. Their parents and chaperones too were impressed with this plan. None of them had ever done anything like it and the young people spoke excitedly about what would happen tonight, while the chaperones looked on with trepidation.

As they proceeded toward the Grand Canal, only about thirty feet from the hotel, they were accosted by the local children who danced around them, alarming some of the Englishmen.

"This is not a problem," said Fabio. "This is indeed part of our custom. We dance as you dance around a Maypole, but you are the Maypole!" With this, the parents relaxed somewhat, and continued on to their waiting fleet of gondolas.

Climbing aboard was a tricky maneuver but eventually all of them were seated safely in the crafts. Once everyone was aboard, the ferrymen - or gondoliers - pushed away from the shore with their long poles. The group of boats moved effortlessly through the crystalline waters of the Grand Canal from the Ponte di Rialto to the Piazza San Marco. They briefly traveled out into the lagoon, before turning and mooring by the Doge's Palace. There was already a crowd of about sixty other revelers who had arrived before them from other hotels, and the group from the Serenissima Hotel huddled together not knowing quite how to behave. This was new to all of them.

However, as soon as they reached the St. Mark's Square, they felt liberated from their worry and fear. The entire square was divided from the citizens of Venice, and a dance floor had been installed before the string orchestra made up of a number of violins and 'cellos, as well as a phalanx of archlutes who were playing merry music of a most rustic nature. The youthful crowd were filled with joy at the prospect of a dance, and the young lady closest to Emma, a girl from London named Melissa, spoke to her.

"I say, Emma, do you think we could be asked to dance by the local gentry?" and here she indicated the rustic band of youths who were approaching them at a trot. "They do look quite uncivilized," she added.

"Yes they do," said Emma, although she was mightily impressed with the pairs of well-shaped legs that were attached to these rustic-costumed youths. There were about forty young men shyly approaching, heads down. One in particular, sporting a large curling moustache approached Emma and her heart leapt into her throat. Melissa, seeing this coarse display, bravely put herself between them, but the youth had other things on his mind. He deftly danced to the side and continued toward Emma.

"Mia Colombina," he said bravely. "I would like to request the honor of the next dance."

Emma had attended many balls and never had she had such a brazen request. The dance card seemed to have failed to cross the Alps and his strange request was met with her silence. She looked down, shyly, following the dictates of her leaping heart, and the ancient saying "when in Rome, do as the Romans do." Then she raised her head and responded with a hearty "I would be honored!"

This response seemed to take the youth by surprise, but his face, under the mask, lit up. "Allow me," he said, brazenly taking her hand, to the shock and astonishment of the other young English women. Emma proceeded, with this young man, to the dance floor and began to dance a new continental dance they called a Valse. Before she knew what was happening, their hands touched as they went through the intricate steps of this scandalously close dance, and each time his soft fingers graced hers, she blushed. In moments, she was transported to a time and a place many years and miles from her own and she smiled and began to enjoy herself. He brushed closer to her and smiled. He had a most bewitching smile; his lips were full and red and his teeth quite perfect. His eyes, blue as the sea, were dancing with joy and he was clearly entranced by her beauty. She thought she saw his eyes dance over her décolleté collar, and she decided to taunt him by bending lower, and smiling as she went through the steps with this mystery man. When the dance stopped, she smiled, thanked him and turned on her heel. He looked crestfallen.

 Emma returned to the brood of young English women, enjoying the astonishment of the majority, and as Melissa approached her, she smiled.

 "You are the bravest lass in all the world," said Melissa. "Dancing a Waltz with that brute!" She smiled jealously at Emma, and Emma noticed that her own mother was enjoying a refreshment at a series of tables that had been set up on the other side of the dance floor. She was watching Emma carefully, and smiling approvingly. Emma, emboldened by this reaction, looked about for other dance partners, realizing that she had impressed the young Italians. The youth who had danced with her was surrounded by a group of young men who were laughing and smiling excitedly. Perhaps she had made a shameful display, but not knowing the rules, she decided to approach the table of wine glasses filled with a sparkling wine and refresh herself. A young Englishman reached for a glass and proffered it smiling.

"May I have the pleasure of this dance with you, Miss Colombina?" he said, in a passable Italian pronunciation.

"I would be delighted," she said bravely, taking his arm and returning to the dance floor, that had now been filled with partners enjoying the magic of the candlelit dusk.

Her nameless English dance partner, dressed, as all the young men were, as Arlecchino, had none of the grace of the young Italian gentleman, and her Quadrille was a near disaster, as he nearly stepped upon her red shoes, kicking up dust and soiling them in the process. Emma, deftly avoided disaster, but resolved not to dance with this dunce again. When the dance ended, she applauded politely with her gloved hand and turned to the Italian throng. The young man with the mustachio saw her, and darted out toward her.

"I see you can dance even with the most club-footed varlet," he said, laughing.

"You were watching, I see," she said. "That was an excruciating experience, and you simply must dance with me now, to take away the shame."

He smiled and approached her, close, and she could feel his breath on her cheek. "I would be delighted," he murmured.

Out on the dance floor, a Valse began again, as though by the design of Cupid. They danced again, touching hands, and smiling at one another. The impossibility of knowing who this mystery man was, was so alluring and entrancing that she could scarcely maintain her decorum. He approached her repeatedly, with a deft dance step and she danced around him just as agile as he.

After the dance ended, the mustachioed youth bowed low to her, as she hid her masked face from his with her fan. She was excited in a way she had never been excited, and felt as though she may swoon. Seeing this, the youth snatched a flute from the wine table and brought it to her to refresh herself. The taste was delightful and the bubbles tickled her masked nose.

"This is a wondrous elixir," she said, laughing, and feeling abandon take over her soul.

"This is called prosecco," he said proudly. "L'elisir d'amore." Emma did not speak Italian but with the wine in her she suddenly knew precisely what he was talking about. This was how people felt when they fell in love! And the anonymity of it was scandalous and at the same time so exciting that she could barely contain herself.

A Foreign Affair

She took his hand. "Dance with me again, my Arlecchino," she demanded, and the youth, who needed no more enticement, took her by the hand and led her to the dance floor. Dancing was more of a challenge by this point, and she felt lighter on her feet than she had ever felt. "I am in heaven," she kept repeating to herself, as she danced, admiring the legs of the masked mustachioed man. Before she knew it, he had whisked her to a far part of the dance floor, and as suddenly as if she were dropped from a window, she felt a pair of warm and thick lips on hers. Eagerly, she kissed him back, forgetting herself entirely, and she felt this kiss go through her body like an arrow from the quiver of Cupid. She eagerly kissed him back, and pulled him to her.

"I am in heaven," she finally said out loud. He laughed quietly, but kissed her again and again. She would have been scandalized but something was making her continue. Maybe it was the twinkling lights, maybe it was the crepuscular light, maybe it was the strangeness of the foreign affair, but she wanted this man with all her heart.

Emma knew that she had fallen into a new world that had broken all decorum and none of the things she had held on to in her life mattered anymore. She felt his hands on her neck, and she kissed him fervently, almost desperately. This moment had to be held on to in order to have it continue. He felt it too and she heard him whisper in her ear. "My English angel, I wish to marry you. Please, can I meet you tomorrow by the Rialto Bridge. My name is Federico Zane, and I am a nobleman from the Venetian gentry. But I want you with all my heart."

"Federico Zane," she repeated. "You are my heart, darling." and she kissed him once again. And then she looked up, to see her mother approaching. Perhaps she had seen something, and feared for her daughter. Maybe she had simply needed to reassure herself that all was well, but for whatever reason, Emma suddenly felt guilty and terrible that she had let herself be transported by her emotions in such a brazen way. Had this been English, her reputation should have been ruined. "Please, Federico, she said. "Take me back to the dance."

Seeing the elder woman approaching, he realized what had happened and swiftly took her by the hand, as innocently as if he were a child and he led her to the dance floor.

"My apologies for taking liberties my dear," he said. "But please, for the sake of all the angels in heaven, allow me to know who you are."

"I am Emma Shaftesbury," she declared bravely, and he smiled.

"Are you related to Donna Anne Shaftesbury?" he asked.

"She is my mother," said Emma.

"In that case, we shall meet again," he said. "I must go," and he was gone in the crowd of Arlecchinos. Emma searched the crowd for him but he was lost; and she was forlorn, unable to see him amid the sea of identically dressed dancing figures.

Emerging as though from a dream, Emma spied her mother approaching and, more dead than alive, she moved to her. "Mother, I must go home," said Emma in a daze. Her mother looked at her with concern, thinking she had been filled with joy and discovering that she was bereft.

"Has something happened?" she asked, concerned.

"No mother," said Emma. "It's just that I have a headache. Mother please, I do not think I can take much more of this dancing and revelry."

"Of course, my dear," said Anne, slightly concerned for her daughter who, up until this point, had never wanted to leave a dance early.

They returned to the hotel aboard a gondola, and the waves calmed their hearts. Emma returned to herself as she sat back on the rocking boat, while Anne calmed her motherly nerves, lulled by the waves.

Chapter 7. The Zanes

The following morning, Anne entered the dining room of their suite with a letter in her hand.

"Emma, I have very good news. I may have told you that many years ago I visited Venice with my father, we stayed for several months as guests of a noble family called the Zanes. They have invited us for lunch today. Would you like to attend?

"Oh mother, will they be speaking in that beastly tongue all the time?"

"Why no, of course not. The Zane family are frequent visitors to England. The reason they hosted my father and I when I visited all those years ago is because they are great Anglophiles and all of them are very fluent in English. Shall I accept their invitation?"

"Yes of course," said Emma rather more eagerly than her mother had expected.

At two in the afternoon, after they had taken the air on the rooftop of the hotel, the two ladies boarded a gondola headed for the villa owned by the noble Zane family.

At the home, they were announced by a footman who helped them disembark from the gondola into their ground level landing area.

"Welcome to the palazzo of the Zanes," he said with a smile.

"Thank goodness you speak English," said Emma.

"Yes. English," he said. "Please to follow me this way." He led them to the second floor, which was where the drawing room was situated. The patriarch of the family stood by the door, leaning casually against the frame. He was a very attractive man with dancing black eyes and a powdered wig adorned with many beautiful curls, in the ancient style. He was dressed in a scarlet velvet and brocade waistcoat and blue breeches, with a well-fitting pair of white stockings, finished by a pair of fashionable high-heeled shoes. In short, he looked the picture of the eighteenth-century gentleman. When he saw, Anne, he bowed deeply and with great solemnity. As he rose, he approached and kissed Anne's hand, without saying a word. Anne blushed and laughed softly as though remembering something from her past. Emma looked to her mother with a look of confusion and looked back at the gentleman.

"Permit me to introduce you to Michele Zane, condottiere of the Serenissima," said Anne to her daughter. "Signore Zane, allow me to introduce you to my daughter, Emma Shaftesbury."

"I am enchanted," he said with a smile, kissing Emma's hand in the continental style. Just then, a door opened at the far end of the drawing room and a figure clad in modern, and finely tailored long striped pantaloons and a fashionable long waistcoat, with straps under his shoes, a top hat he doffed as soon as he entered the room, revealing a perfectly formed face, with huge dark eyes framed with outlandishly long eyelashes, a perfectly aquiline nose, and full red lips, topped with a brilliant and expertly curled moustache. Of course, Emma recognized her Arlecchino at once, and he recognized his Colombina. She let down her guard by gasping and blushing deeply.

Anne looked at her daughter who appeared to be behaving very badly, and knit her brows, thinking she was being impolite. She nudged Emma for a reaction. Emma looked at her mother, confused.

"Ah, yes," said the elder Zane. "Allow me to introduce my eldest son, Federico, heir to my position in the Most Serene Republic. Or what remains of it, after Napoleon." He laughed hollowly.

"Of course, Michele," said Anne. "Your world must be shattered after that brute came and threw everything into chaos."

"One does what one can," he said.

The son, Federico, stepped forward and kissed Anne's hand. "You are the charming English lady that inspired my father all those years ago."

"Oh, I don't know that that is true," she responded.

"But yes, madam, it is true," said Michele. "For I was educated primarily in English, and I have been very fortunate to visit your island quite frequently. Indeed, we attended the opera in London many times. But madamina, have we met?" he added, looking at Emma. Emma looked at him as though he were mad. Of course they had met. Dear Lord, she had abased herself and kissed this man. How on earth could he be behaving so? She began shyly nodding, nervously looking to him and then to her mother.

"Emma! You must respond," hissed Anne, annoyed at her eldest daughter's lack of manners. "Say something back to him."

Emma cleared her throat. "Thank you, Signore Zane. I believe we may have met under mysterious circumstances. You see, last night, I was dressed as a character named Colombina, who is, I believe, one of your

Commedia dell'arte characters, and so I was disguised. Nevertheless, I believe I recognize your moustache, and I believe we may have danced together, if my mind is not deceiving me."

"Ah, yes, of course," he said, his beautiful eyes dancing. His eyebrows raised high, he smiled. It was almost lascivious. "But father, I have good news. Our box seat at the opera is prepared and ready for the new fascinating opera by a wonderful young composer named Rossini. You must join us!"

"Oh mother!" said Emma, turning to her mother. "I simply must go to the opera in Venice. Please say I can."

"I cannot abide the opera, darling, but if Signore Zane is willing to accompany you, I see no reason why you cannot see it." Clearly, she meant the father, and not wanting to lose her chance at a rendezvous.

"We would be glad to accompany Miss Shaftesbury to the opera," said the elder Zane. "And now, let us adjourn to the dining room; we have prepared a wonderful meal for you of Venetian delicacies."

And indeed, to a sumptuous meal of polenta with wild boar, risotto con funghi, and many desserts that were delicious and tempting, Michele Zane reminisced with Anne about the six months she spent with the Zane family before she was married to Sir Rufus, Emma's father. Emma was scandalized that her mother had been travelling without her father, until she realized that she had been accompanied by a chaperone - her own mother - and that she had yet even to meet Rufus Shaftesbury, her future husband. Anne, perhaps sensing her discomfort with this topic, and pleading a headache, arranged for the two of them to leave before three o'clock. Federico turned to Emma as she donned her overcoat and smiled.

"I shall come to the hotel and fetch you at six. The opera begins at seven and it would be a tragedy to miss the noblemen appearing. It is one of those sights one must take in if one is to understand the Serenissima."

"I shall be ready," said Emma, as the turned to the door, blushing. She felt lightheaded when she looked in Federico Zane's astonishingly beautiful face. It was not at all feminine; it reminded her of the bust of Marcus Aurelius she had seen once, and that they were planning on seeing in Rome. Of course, beards were very unfashionable in that time, but the moustache was similar and his perfect nose was Romanesque in its grandeur. But rather than inspire her to noble thoughts, this living Roman emperor inspired her to think thoughts of love and romance. For Emma Shaftesbury was a thoroughly modern young lady, and her love for romances was considerable. She saw in Federico Zane an exotic man who could sweep her off her feet, or rescue her from a seraglio in Persia, or, if she were not careful, ruin her.

A Foreign Affair

At five-thirty, Emma had roused Nell from her stupor into action, to help her get dressed. "Nell! You have done yeoman service repairing my frock. I simply must look distinguished today too. You know I am going to the opera. "The Barber of Seville" is playing you know."

"Oh ma'am," said Nell. "I 'ad no idea you was gonna get your hair done. Let me give you some combs."

"Whatever are you talking about darling? I am going to the opera, not the hairdressing salon."

"The opera? What's that, then?"

"It's a very distinguished affair, with music and drama, and costumes, and scenery."

"Like the music hall back home? I've sat there of an evening. Very divertin' if I may say so ma'am."

"Not much like that I shouldn't think," said Emma. "The opera is one of the pinnacles of achievement of mankind, Nell, and not a series of entertainers like the music hall performances. Noble writers write verse and distinguished composers set their words to music. You remember the fuss about Mozart? He was such a composer. He made up some very clever operas. And now there is this new genius named Rossini, and he has made up another clever opera called *The Barber of Seville*. Now do you understand?"

"I confess, I never understood much about you sorts of people. You go to watch operas in a language you don't even speak. How is that sensible?"

"It's very highbrow, Nell. One doesn't need to understand the words. The music is its own language. And besides, one goes to see and be seen."

"Ah! I understand it now," said Nell, smiling knowingly. In a few more minutes, the clever ministrations of Nell and her needle rejuvenated Emma's frock, and her brilliant turn with a brush and some carefully applied powder made Emma Shaftesbury look like a grand dame attending the opera for the thousandth time. At least that was the assessment of Anne, just before the gondola appeared at the mooring station of the hotel.

The assessment of Federico Zane, who had appeared without his father, was equally flattering.

"Good evening Madama Shaftesbury," he said with a bow.

Anne Shaftesbury laughed and showed him into the drawing room. "And how is your father, Master Zane?"

"He is quite well, although I feel he may have overtaxed himself today; he says he may have a touch of the ague."

"Oh my goodness," said Anne. "I do hope he has recovered by tomorrow."

"I am sure he will. To be honest, I think it might be the opera. He is more interested in the older *opere serie*, and these humorous turns are not his style. This is music for the young!"

"Well, I trust you will be a safe guardian of Emma. She has never been to the opera and I know there are cads that frequent the opera house!"

"Fear not," said Federico. "I will be with her every minute. Do not worry about that!"

For whatever reason - a slackening of her vigilance, given the trustworthiness of young Emma, the foreignness of all the surroundings, or some other thing that Emma was not privy to, Anne raised no objection to their sallying forth together, unaccompanied. Emma would find out later that her mother had been terribly disoriented, but at the time, Emma rejoiced to be alone with the object of her desire.

Federico turned to her, his blue eyes adoring her. "My plan worked perfectly. We shall be alone, my darling, and we will be able to enjoy the opera." Emma's heart leaped into her mouth at his brazen words.

"Take my hand," he said, as he gently guided her to her seat at the back of the gondola. "Will you allow me to sit beside you?"

"I would wish nothing more!" she replied.

He took his place beside her, holding her hand firmly.

They set off across the canal, and south to the Piazza San Marco, around the lagoon to La Fenice Theater. Most of the gondolas had not yet begun to appear, and so they were able to secure a grand space to make fast. Federico, greeting many of his friends in Italian, helped Emma out of the craft and guided her along the hallway to the main meeting room of the famous theater.

As she walked down the hall accompanied by Federico, she nearly fainted. "It is too beautiful to be believed!" she said.

"Yes," said Federico. "This is one of the grandest theater's in Europe. And one of the newest. Someone burned it down about thirty years ago, but, as we Venetians often say 'com'era, dov'era.'"

"Forgive me, Federico, but I am not Italian. What does 'camera dovera' mean?"

He laughed to hear her accent. "Yes of course," he said. "Forgive me, Emma. 'Com'era', means 'as it was' and 'dov'era' means 'where it was'. So it is rebuilt exactly where the old theater was and exactly like the theater. You see?"

"I do," she enthused. "It is more beautiful than anything I have ever seen."

"They say it is a jewel box," he said, smiling.

To say it was grand would not do it justice; it was beautiful and almost brand new. It had been built in 1774 after the first theater in this spot had burnt to the ground.

"What is called?" she asked

"La Fenice," he said. Then he laughed. "This is irony, Venetian style," said Federico. "Since it means phoenix, the firebird that rose from the ashes."

"I should say the irony is hardly the most interesting thing about this building," she said. "It is the horror of a whole theater engulfed in flames, and then the ingenuity of the builders to restore it as it was."

"I think you have a good point," he said, taking her hand as he led her into the main auditorium.

"Dear God, that chandelier is massive!"

"Yes," he said. "They say it is illuminated by thousands of candles, reflected by thousands upon thousands of crystals, and burnished gold arms. But we have a loggia!" he added, taking her to a corridor off the side of the theater.

"Do we not have seats?" she asked.

"Of course. In fact, the family has a whole little room. Come!" and he led her to a beautifully appointed little room that was screened in and totally private. She looked down at the theater, and suddenly felt safe, but somehow strange; while she could see everything that was happening on stage, and certainly could watch the audience who were seated in the public seats, her seat, upon an ornately painted beech chair, painted gold with beautiful white brocade seat cushions. There were two seats that could be used to sit and watch the opera, but there was also a chaise longue behind it that seemed to have other, less honorable uses.

"Please, Miss Shaftesbury," said Federico as he motioned for her to take a seat at the front of the box. "The opera will begin in a few minutes. The orchestra practices with some solo singers whom we can enjoy, or, perhaps we could meet some of the Venetian nobles; they are a very aristocratic lot."

Emma, who had never been exposed to this sort of personal chatter from a relative stranger, did not really know how to react, and so she looked quite panicked and turned away from this man who was exposing her to so many new experiences, and coughed quietly. "I think I'll stay with the musicians, thank you."

Federico, sensing that something was wrong, leapt down to the lower level and took her hand in his. "Miss Shaftesbury, you misunderstand me. I would never try to put you in an uncomfortable position. Please,

A Foreign Affair

dear lady, let us enjoy the performance here in the privacy of our box."

"Is it really entirely private?" she asked.

"I have locked the door," he said, showing her the key which he then slipped into his pocket. For a moment, Emma felt trapped, but as she looked at his long and beautiful eyelashes, and the kind look on his face, and that magnificent moustache, she felt something akin to joy. This was, in fact, what all the dances and billet-doux, and every chance encounter, dinner, or event in the capital was intended to bring to her. And here he is, of his own free will, separate from the prying and judgmental eyes of her mother or father, alone. It was astonishing. It was scandalous, but it was also quite perfect.

Emma felt a strong urge to lean over and kiss him, although she resisted the urge strongly. She was properly brought up, after all, and knew better than to ruin herself. She had read enough romances where the heroine ruins herself over an indiscretion such as this. But the urge to destruction ran through her body like a herd of wild horses, and she could feel her heart beating against her ribs like a prisoner banging on the iron bars of his cell. She was feeling an overwhelming sense that things were disorienting and discomfiting but she also could not and would not change a thing for the world. She felt Federico's attentive hand, warm and soft, almost feminine, and yet strong and large, in hers. She could feel his breath on her, and she felt as though she may swoon.

As the opera began, she began to feel better. The overture was very beautiful, very fast, and very interesting. It immediately seized her attention and held it almost as though she were transported to another world.

"Who is this Rossini?" asked Emma. "I have never heard of him or his work."

Beaming, Federico looked at her, and said "Rossini is a young man, in his twenties;

he is really one of us, a youth. He writes beautifully don't you find?"

"It is honestly like nothing I have ever heard," said Emma. "I find myself laughing at these witticisms, and I can barely understand a word of what he says."

"Then you can imagine what brilliance there is in his work for the Italian audience. I must say, he has taken the world by storm. I think he will be one of our greatest composers. And I am so glad I could experience this with you."

Confused, Emma looked at Federico. "Have you seen this opera before?"

"Of course," he said. "I go every night. Many of my friends are in love with Anna Renzi, the soprano, but I, of course, only have eyes for one beauty." His eyes twinkled as he spoke and she felt his hand squeeze hers. As the hand squeezed her hand, her heart leapt out of her body, filled with joy. She had the strongest urge of her life, to kiss this man. And then, she remembered the kiss she and he shared last night. As this happened, a feeling of calm descended over her, and she sat back, smiling. The singers on the stage were running from room to room, slamming doors, and singing at the top of their lungs, and mayhem was everywhere. This was a new world for Emma, and a great world it was. It was a world she wanted to be part of, and this man was the one she wanted to marry.

As soon as this thought crossed her mind, she checked herself. She was an English woman and she needed to remember that she had certain duties and obligations, and these did not involve the sort of careless thoughts that let her lose herself. Knitting her brows, Emma crossed her arms, and felt Federico's soft hands on her forearm, and she could feel the heat that was burning through her sleeve. She was falling, she could tell, and she was falling very hard, and inextricably for this beautiful youth with the shapely legs and the long eyelashes and the manly moustache. Breathless, she sighed as she glanced at him, seeing him beam back at her, and it was clear that they were both enjoying the opera.

At the interval, she rose and looked forward to leaving the box, to enjoy some refreshment. As she passed by the chaise longue, she noticed that there was a bowl of delicious fruits sitting there, enticingly. She looked to Federico, who leapt to the door, holding it for her and she exited.

"I have arranged for you to have some prosecco," he said, leading the way to the vendor at the stall outside in the lobby. The place was loud and boisterous with young and attractive people chattering away in all the possible languages. She could make out French and English, German, and Italian in the crowd. Emma was surprised that the assembled multitudes were such a Babel, and that they were so young and vigorous. Many of the young men were looking flirtatiously at some of the young women. There were two kinds of older women – fashionably dressed women who were discoursing on the compositional technique of the composer, and of the political ramifications of the libretto, or so Federico told her, and a group of demure, black-clad women who were silent as the tomb and appeared to be having no fun at all.

"Tell me about the society here," asked Emma, inquisitively.

"Well, as you know, Venice is the city of the Cortigiana." He looked at Emma with a smile. Emma said nothing for a minute, and when she realized that he was not going to go on, she looked to him and said "What, pray, is a cortigiana?"

"You see these fashionable and learned women?" he said. Emma nodded.

"Cortigiani," he said, matter-of-factly.

"I suppose that they are the dandies of Italian society," she said.

"Well they are the arbiters of taste. They are what you call courtesans in English. Ladies of easy virtue in some cases, and ladies of great learning and accomplishment in others. But they are forever fashionable. Even out own Anna Renzi is a courtesan."

"You mean the soprano?" asked Emma.

"I do," he said.

Emma was shocked but she was also fascinated by the liberation inherent in this as-yet – to her – unknown class of people. They seemed so forward thinking and free; they were inspiring to her.

"You know, Federico," said Emma. "I would very much like to return to our box, but this time, I would like to sit on the chaise longue and enjoy some of the fruit I saw there."

Federico's eyes lit up. "Of course," he said, leading her along the aisle to the little cloth covered door that led to their loggia. As he led her along the passage, he put his hand on the small of her back, sensing her comfort with his familiarity. He was hoping to find another time to steal a kiss, and now that she knew about courtesans, she knew that there was a world of intimate and infinite possibility.

In the box, she sat back and listened to the music wash over her as she ate grapes fed to her by the adoring young courtier. He sat deftly on the table as she lay back on the chaise, and his hand grasped hers in a fervent expression of closeness. Emma closed her eyes as she tasted these delicious grapes, enjoyed the feeling of his hand in hers, and let the music wash over them.

"I am in heaven," she said, feeling as though she had said it before. And in many ways, this was the greatest moment of her life up to that point. The brilliant music, the stunning costumes, the company which was perfect for her, and everything which was more perfect than she could have imagined, worked together to convince her that she had found her perfection.

On the ride back to the hotel, Emma sat in the gondola, illuminated by a candelabra of beautiful candles. She trailed one hand in the canal, as the gondolier poled his way along the Grand Canal while her young suitor sang her an arietta from the opera.

> Ecco ridente in cielo spunta la bella aurora,
> e tu non sorgi ancora e puoi dormir così?
> Sorgi, mia dolce speme, vieni bell'idol mio,
> rendi men crudo, oh Dio, lo stral che mi feri.
> Oh sorte! già veggo quel caro sembiante,
> quest'anima amante ottenne pietà!
> Oh, istante d'amore! Felice momento!
> Oh, dolce content che egual non ha!

"Oh, Federico," said Emma. "Tell me what you are singing about."

Federico put her hand to his lips, and pulled her close. Emma smiled. "It is about the dawn breaking and his love is still asleep."

"Tell me more!" she said, a tear in her eye.

"Well, of course this lover, he wants her to wake up to soften the pain from Cupid's arrow."

"How romantic!" said Emma, her breath getting shorter.

"Yes," said Federico. "And then, he sees his lover, because she has taken pity on his soul. And, dear Emma, what this man experiences is a moment of love, that divine moment which is unparalleled."

Emma felt she may swoon at the beauty of his conversation. "Oh please sing it again," she said, and as he sang, the love he felt was transmitted to her directly as a form of poetry she could never have duplicated. After several minutes on the gondola, looking out at the twinkling lights of the other candlelit gondolas, the larger craft, and the lights in the windows of the palazzi, she sighed and turned to Federico. He smiled back.

"Madamina," he began.

"Please," said Emma. "Call me Emma."

"Emma then," he said, smiling broadly. "I have never felt this way before. I have ridden on the Grand Canal thousands of times, and never have I seen the stars fall from the skies into the waters, and never have I seen them reflected in another's eyes in such a profound way. I daresay I am afraid to say more."

"Say more," sighed Emma. "For I feel the same thing you do. It is as though we are constellations, like Orpheus and Eurydice."

Federico was smitten before but when he heard the wisdom and beauty of Emma's words, he melted. "Emma," he continued. "I want so much to ask your hand."

Emma was shocked at this admission. Although she herself was transported and was willing to tell him, she knew it was wrong and unfair to try to take advantage of him in this way. At some level she was torn, because she wanted to feel his lips on hers, but she knew that society would shun her forever, and she would never be able to bring herself back.

"Please, my dear Federico," said Emma, noting that she had made pains to pronounce his name correctly, and seeing that he approved. "Do not say another word. You have said too much already. As have I."

Federico looked devastated. His face lost its pallor and he was weakened. He sat back on the seat and contemplated her words. They were nearing the hotel landing just at the moment.

The gondolier began to sing a boat song, softly and tenderly, and Federico took this moment, knowing he would never be able to do it again, and kissed Emma tenderly and fervently, desperately and passionately. She kissed him back and her hand squeezed his. She opened her passionate mouth and he felt her beautiful and white teeth on his tongue. But even as they were about to lose themselves, the gondola bumped against the pier, and the gondolier stopped their passion with a return to reality.

"Here we are," he said, in Italian. Emma, shocked, pushed Federico away, although every fiber of her being wanted to take him in her arms and kiss him again. "How dare you!" she said stentoriously.

Shocked, Federico shrank from her. "discolpa me, madamina," he said, reverting to Italian, but catching himself. "I did not mean to offend."

"And yet you did!" she said acting as insulted as though she had been robbed. "And now, I would like some assistance in getting to my room, thank you!"

With that, she stepped out of the gondola and turned on her pretty heel, and stormed off, leaving Federico confused and desperate in the seat of the gondola.

The gondolier looked at him and smiled. "Inglese?" he said.

"Certo, certo," said Federico. "Allora, andiamo, a la casa." And with that, without looking at the disappearing back of Emma Shaftesbury, he returned home.

Later that night, by candle light, Federico could be seen in his chambers, writing a letter, steeped in passion and despair. He had several crumpled pieces of paper on the floor around him as though he had been trying in vain to express himself effectively. Shortly, he emerged from his room, with an envelope dripping with his seal, and handed it to the footman.

"This must go to Signora Emma Shaftesbury who is staying at the Serenissima Hotel. I want it delivered as soon as possible."

"But master," protested the lazy servant. "It is the middle of the night."

"And if she does not receive it before dawn breaks, I shall be dead!" he pronounced fervently.

Hearing this, the footman scampered off, through the narrow alleys of the Merceria, to deliver the billet-doux to Miss Shaftesbury.

Wending his way through the dark streets, he felt fear as he had never felt fear before. This was the first time his young master had demanded that he go out at night and he had heard tales of thieves and prostitutes who filled the alleys. Periodically, he was heartened by the Prie-Dieu, with their little candles, that brightened his journey.

A Foreign Affair

He heard voices inside the houses of many of the residents, but never once did he encounter another. He was surprised but he also noted that the cathedral, located far off across the lagoon, was tolling three o'clock. It was dark and moonless, and he was fearful that he would lose his way. Nevertheless, with the surety of a life-long Venetian, he found the Serenissima Hotel very quickly and delivered the letter to the bellhop in the lobby.

After a short conversation and the exchange of a few small coins, the letter made its way up the stairs to the second floor and the table upon which Miss Shaftesbury's visitors would deposit their calling cards.

All night long, Federico stayed awake, with terror in his heart, his heart aching with the joy of a new-found love. Little did he know that at the Serenissima Hotel, Emma, who had stormed off with such mock-indignation, was floating on air. She was absolutely in love, and wanted nothing more or less than to fly out her window across the canal to the house of the Zanes, and rap gently on his window, be admitted, and have her lover ravish her.

She lay in the bed, smiling with joy, forgetting entirely that her lover was bereft, thinking he had ruined their budding romance. She was merely behaving as she knew she must when a gentleman took liberties; but for the Italian, unaccustomed to this behavior, she had shunned him.

If Federico Zane could only see her now, as she glowed with new-found adoration of her swarthy lover, he would not be so downhearted. No, he would be writing a letter asking permission of her father, and not a letter of abject apology.

Unable to sleep, Emma rose from her little bed and opened the door where the table of calling cards was situated. She hoped to see something there, but seeing nothing, she returned to the drawing room.

She sighed and flung herself on the divan, watching the candlelight glinting on the gentle waves of the canal. This was a city of such beauty that she was almost incapable of taking it in. She momentarily considered that perhaps she had mistaken the enchantment she felt for her young suitor with her enchantment of the city, but then she recalled his red lips and his passion, his long eyelashes and his huge eyes that captured the seas.

'No,' she told herself, 'this was the love that comes but once in a lifetime.' And she, Emma Shaftesbury, had found it here in the jewel box city, in this city of canals, in the greatest drawing room in Europe.

And then about half past three in the morning, she went back to the little anteroom that housed the table, and saw the billet-doux sitting on the table. Rushing into the room, she took it and read the inscription: "Madamina Emma Shaftesbury, by hand," and she looked at the seal which was GZ.

"Emma:" it read. "I have done a terrible harm to you," he wrote.

"What is he talking about?" she thought. "How can he think he did me harm?" She read on:

> "I have taken advantage and owe you a great and profound apology. What can I do to beg your forgiveness? What can I offer as restitution?"

Emma was flustered; she had expected to read a letter declaring his love, but then this letter appeared, and she realized she had behaved abominably. She had treated this man who loved her as though he were a pest. What kind of person was she? She needed to see him, she needed to ask his forgiveness. But of course, she did not know the streets and she had no gondola, and so she had no choice but to write a letter and have it delivered by hand as he had done.

> "Dearest Federico:" she wrote. "Nay, you owe me nothing, for it was I who misled you. I want you to forgive me

for misbehaving, for letting myself be a petulant child, for I do love you with all my heart. And I am not afraid to say it. Forgive me, come back to me, and love me, nay marry me, Federico! I will accept, and I believe my father will too. Please forgive my stupidity. Return before we leave or my heart will break.

"I leave you with my address in Kent, in case we have to leave first. I am, as you know, under the control and care of my mother, who has her heart set on giving me the Grand Tour, and never counted on letting me go out unchaperoned. Nor, may I say, did she ever think we would fall in love. Dare I say that? Dearest, I still want to marry you but I know how difficult a road we have ahead of us. Let me ask you, nay invite you to come to my home in Kent and ask my father for my hand. Do come, dearest Federico, do come and we can be forever together in a love that has never been matched. I love you with all my heart and all my soul. Yours, Emma Shaftesbury."

She sealed the envelope, and took the candle, daubing the wax to seal the lip of the letter. Then she flew out the door and down to the lobby without noting that she wore her night dress, which was, admittedly a beautiful white empire-waist gown, and bare foot. As she reached the front desk in the lobby of the hotel, she banged her fist on the bell, causing a bright alarm to toll throughout the darkened area. There was a rustling from the back room and a small scruffy lad appeared with a taper in his hand.

"Che?" said the bleary-eyed lad.

Suddenly, Emma realized that her inability to speak Italian was going to cause her some trouble.

"Per favore," she said drawing on every word she knew of the Italian tongue. "Io voglio che tu prenderà la lettera alla casa Zane. Can you do that?"

The little ruffian nodded. "La casa Zane? Certo."

"Bless you!" she said, dropping several small coins in his hand. She watched his eyes light up and he snatched the letter and tore off down a back street at breakneck speed. Emma smiled, knowing she was in good hands. Suddenly exhausted with mental energy and physical exertion, she trudged up the stairs and went to sleep.

Chapter 8. The Cad

In the morning, Emma begged her mother to stay in bed for the morning, and her mother, believing she may have caught the ague, agreed. Anne decided to go out into the Merceria, the shopping district and summoned Nell to accompany her.

"Now Nell, I am certain you will not find this as edifying as the opera, but I would be grateful if you would accompany me to the shopping district. Would you be so kind?"

"What opera, ma'am?" said Nell confused.

"The opera you attended with Emma, of course," she said nonchalantly.

"I didn't attend no opera ma'am," said Nell. "And thank the Good Lord for that, anyway. I could never abide them shriekers. But I would love to come to the shops with you. Even if I could never afford a thing."

Anne was confused, thinking she had attended with Emma, but decided not to pursue the issue. Some things were better not pursued.

She donned her overcoat, and dragging Nell with her, she made her way to the Merceria, where there were displays of the most beautiful garments she had ever seen. Some of these made the clothing in Paris look positively threadbare.

Turning a corner, she was nearly overwhelmed by the sea of eager shopping faces. The street was narrow and filled with all manner of people. She held her purse close to her chest, and avoided the eyes of any of the rough characters who were hanging around many of the corners. At one corner, she caught sight of a familiar jacket, and as she turned to Nell, she said "Is that not the young Zane boy?"

"Who's that, ma'am?" said Nell, looking the wrong way.

Anne pointed at the direction of the young man who seemed to be in the company of a young woman. She squinted and looked closer. Although she would never admit it,

Anne was very near-sighted, and had very little confidence in her ability to see what she needed to see.

"Look carefully," said Anne, nudging Nell.

Nell leaned forward. "If I can be tot'ly honest, mum, these Eye-talians look all the same to me. I have no idea at all for distinguishing them. But that young man is taking liberties, is what I can tell you."

Anne was shocked. She looked carefully, and began to move through the crowd in the direction of this young man. "If that is young Federico Zane, and I believe it is, then there is a something frightful happening. You must know that my daughter is quite smitten."

"That I know, mum," said Nell.

"And, well, this would be a scandal. And one we must investigate." She was nudging people through the crowd, and pushing and elbowing in a most unladylike way, earning the wrath of several gentlemen.

"I say, madam!" said one young dandy, who added "These Italians have no manners at all."

"I am an Englishwoman and I have business here, young man."

"Well, you have a want of manners, milady," said the cad.

Anne decided to disregard his comment and moved toward the young man who appeared to be stealing a kiss from a young lady. However, the closer she got, the less she could tell where she was going. Moments after this altercation, she had lost the young Zane boy.

"Nell, I have resolved that we must be on our way. We must get a coach to take us to away from here. This city has far too many temptations. We must away! Do me the honor of finding us a coach that will transport us as soon as possible to the next destination. I care not if it is Florence or Rome."

"Yes, ma'am," said Nell. She hurried off in the direction of the Rialto Bridge, where all the transportation was located.

Anne, thoroughly confused by the morning's traffic, hurried back to the hotel.

She entered the hotel room, where her daughter was now awake and dressed. "Emma, my dear, we really must leave here at the earliest opportunity. I have asked Nell to secure transport for us away from here. Could you prepare yourself for a journey? Have you sufficiently recovered?"

Emma looked at her mother who appeared to be very disturbed. "Mother," she said slowly. "What has happened? Were you accosted by a villain in the Merceria?"

"Oh no," said Anne, laughing. "It is nothing of the kind. It is simply that we really need to be on our way. There are many treasures to be viewed and appreciated on our journey, and I have been shirking my duties when it comes to your education."

"Oh mother. There is nothing to worry about. I have learned more in these two months than in all my time at finishing school."

"Silly girl," said Anne. "You know you never went to finishing school!"

Emma laughed. "No, mother, I didn't and yet look at how well finished I am. I positively shine!"

Anne laughed, relieved that her daughter was not upset. What she didn't know was that Emma had written a letter and had it delivered to Federico Zane, giving her address back in England. It was for this reason that Emma was so calm; she had set in motion the romance that she so wanted. And behind her mother's back!

In Emma's mind she had done nothing wrong; she had simply responded to a letter from a family friend, which is, according to the rules of civil society, the proper thing to do. The fact that she had not mentioned this to her mother was neither here nor there, she told herself. But if the Good Lord were to shine on her, and answer her fervent prayers, she would be granted her wish: marriage to a swarthy Italian nobleman who had stolen her heart the moment he stole a kiss, dressed as a harlequin. It was simply too brilliant: a genesis story like that would be something they could dine out on for a lifetime.

Emma smiled at her mother. "Mother, I am prepared to move whenever you wish. Just say the word and I shall be on the move."

"I am so relieved, Emma," said Anne. "I confess I was a trifle worried that you would become attached to that Federico Zane lad."

"Why ever would you be worried about that, mother?" she asked.

"Forgive me, Emma, but I sometimes let my imagination run away with me. I should know better than to trust in my feminine side," said Anne, shaking her head in dismay. "And today I let my emotions get the better of me again, for as we were walking in the Merceria, I could have sworn I saw that young devil in the company of another young lady."

As Anne said this, Emma's face fell. "I beg your pardon, mother?" she said.

"Well, you know how poor my sight is, darling," said Anne. But she knew she had said something terribly damaging. "I was sure at first, but as I got closer, I was unsure, and Nell, poor dear, she saw nothing of the kind. Of course I fear her eyes were on the workmen who were tipping their cloth caps at her."

But Emma heard none of this. To say she was devastated would be an understatement. She was bereft. She could not retrieve her letter and yet she had given her heart to this ... lothario.

She fled from the room, and flung herself on her bed, tears staining the sheets. 'What can I do now? Is this even true? Granted,' she thought, 'mother is nearsighted, but mamma had seen *something* and Federico Zane *had* taken liberties with me.

At that moment, Nell ran into the room. "Miss Emma," she said, out of breath.

"I have a letter from the young Eye-talian," she said.

"Oh Nell," she said through a veil of tears. "I am heartbroken. If Federico responds, how will I ever know if he has betrayed my trust?"

Nell handed her the letter, which was, indeed, addressed from Federico Zane. She recognized his seal at once. Her heart stopped as she broke the seal.

"My darling," it began. Emma, in her sadness, noted that it was not specifically addressed to her. It could as easily have been delivered to that young woman in the street. Nevertheless, she went on reading.

> "I was so happy to receive your letter, and your address in England. Let me be perfectly clear: I am yours and I will have you if you would have me. This love you speak of is reciprocated and I add to your love. I shall love you until I die, many years from now, married and happy. Meet me before you leave,

my darling, so I may have one kiss to build this dream upon. I am yours, in honesty and devotion, Federico Zane, Veneziano nobile."

"But Nell," said a confused and heartbroken Emma. "Mother told me she saw him in the Merceria, taking liberties with another young woman."

"You must know how faulty your mother's eyes are," said Nell. "She saw nothing of the kind. I tell you in all honesty, she saw a costume in the shop window, of a Harlequin, and mistook it for your Eye-talian lover boy."

Emma smiled knowingly. "Yes, I see," she said. Snatching a leaf of paper, she flew to her desk and wrote a very quick note.

"My dearest love," she wrote, in imitation of her lover who dared not to use her name.

"I die for you, for my mother does not approve of our union. She has ordered a coach to take me from you. I shall go to Florence or to Rome and thence back to England. You must write to me in England, or, if you are resourceful, write to the best hotel in Florence or Rome. I am yours if you do the labors of Hercules for me. I will give my heart to you, if only we can make the connection. For I confess, I do love you, and I want so very much to have you for my husband. I am yours, evermore, Emma Shaftesbury."

She quickly folded the paper and thrust it at Nell. "Could you, would you deliver this for me darling Nell?" said Emma with desperation. "I shall be in our debt forever if you could do this for me."

"I shall fly to him for you," said Nell, showing strong emotion for the first time in Emma's experience.

Emma smiled at her. "You are my savior, darling Nell. Fly to him for me!"

And without a second glance, Nell flew out the door and down the stairs.

Only moments later, a valet knocked on the door. "Your coach will-a be waiting at the landing in an hour," he said.

Anne was beside herself without Nell. "How on earth can we meet the coach without Nell?" she said breathlessly.

"She will be back in five minutes," said Emma calmly, gathering her things into a pile, addressing the valet who still stood at the door, apparently basking in the glory of his English pronunciation. He appeared to be taken aback that he was being addressed by a young woman, so brazen, and so English.

He looked at her uncomprehending. "I beg your pardon?" he said haltingly.

"I said, she will return in five minutes. Would you be so good as to help us take our bags to the lobby?"

"Of course, madam," he said, snapping to attention, grasping several of the bags, and charging out of the door.

And indeed, Nell was back in moments, without a letter. "I had no time to wait for a response," she said breathlessly.

"Nell," said Anne. "Thank God you've arrived. Wherever have you been?"

Nell looked at Emma, whose eyes, saucers, begged for her silence. "I was visiting a friend," she said.

"Well we are to be on the coach at the landing in less than an hour, my dear," said Anne.

Within an hour, they were seated in a coach, bound for Rome.

Nell leaned to Emma and whispered in her ear. "He said he would write to every hotel in Rome. He said he loves with all his 'eart."

"Bless you, my dear," said Emma, leaning back and closing her eyes, falling fast asleep in minutes.

Chapter 9. Letters from Away

"Dear Federico:" (wrote Emma at the first stop on the journey to Rome): "I must confess that I have been an inferior traveler of late. As we left the city of Venice on the coach that was filled with Italian revelers, and felt something as though I were in some scene from *The Decameron*, I let my head rest against my mother's urgent shoulder. She wanted me to see every last blade of grass on the Appian Way, and I must confess, that, once I had found love, I had no further desire to see any of the glories of Rome, where so many dreadful things were done in the name of civilization.

"In truth, all I really desire at this point is to find you in England, asking my father for my hand. For I have nothing to live for but you and my love is, as Mr. Shakespeare would have said, "as boundless as the sea." God grant me the rest so that I can sleep and dream and perhaps see you there, waiting for me, patiently and lovingly. I remember the feel of your hand on my hand, and your lips on my lips, and I have no other desire of any kind forever and ever. Just you. We have been in this pension run by some sort of nunnery for the past few hours, and while mother wanted to leave to explore the glories of the fount of all civilization, I had no such desire. I simply wanted to wait for the post to arrive to find you letter. And it failed to arrive. I tell myself that it is nothing, that you are busy, you are confused by my instructions, or that you simply could not afford so many letters. Whatever it turns out to be, I shall have had it covered in my full explanation for your silence. The only thing I did not consider was the possibility that you were no longer interested in me. That I know could never be.

"I trust in you and know that one day all will be better. I remain yours, ever, Emma."

It was with a heavy heart that Emma sent Nell out into the coursing streets of the Eternal City to post the letter, all the while wondering if she was simply a fool for love.

Unaccustomed to keeping secrets from her mother, Emma felt a weight on her shoulders that she normally did not feel. She hoped beyond hope that Federico would remember to send her letter to Rome. It was possible that he had sent letters only to the expensive hotels, and not to the small *pensiones*. Regardless, she knew that the transport of letters in Italy was second only to the delivery of mail in England. She had great faith that in a matter of days she could look forward to a missive. And since nothing could be done, she found her mother and begged her to take her to see the glories of Rome.

"Mother, I have been remiss, and I want to be clear that every one of Rome's treasures is something I need to see. I want to see the Sistine Chapel and St. Peter's, as well as the Trevi Fountain."

"Why Emma, I am so relieved to see that you are quite yourself again. I was about to call for the apothecary to see if you could be revived. To what do I owe this joy?"

"I was being a fool, mother. I know I have no hope of marrying an Italian, as charming as that young Zane chap was."

"I was a trifle disturbed about that I must confess, but I have reason for my apprehension about the Zane family."

"What do you mean? Is it a tragic story?"

"Well, no. Not exactly tragic, but it is a cautionary tale."

"Do tell me it, mother."

"It is a story I had hoped not to ever have to relive. But Federico's father, Michele, was something of a beau of mine many years ago. Of course, it was all a misunderstanding, and my family was horrified when they thought I might be running away to Venice to marry some Italian. None of that ever happened of course, as I came to my senses as soon as I was away from him. But I do remember the pain of heartbreak, as silly as that sounds now from the vantage point of a happily married lady."

Emma was surprised to hear this news, as she had never imagined her mother courting another than her father. With very little to help her understand her mother's experience, she decided to change the subject. "Can we visit the Trevi Fountain first? I do love a fountain," she said.

Anne looked at Emma and smiled. "Ah yes. That is a wonderful idea. You know the legend about the fountain, do you? If you throw one coin in the fountain, you will return to Rome."

"I had heard that one must shy three coins in the fountain to ensure that you will find a new love and marriage."

"I had never heard that legend," said Anne. "Wherever did you hear it?"

"Why, Nell told me it is an ancient legend among the working classes," said Emma.

"Well then, let us go and try our luck. I shall bring some *baiocchi* to toss into the fountain."

"Mother, I have no idea what that is," laughed Emma, joyfully.

"These are *baiocchi*," said Anne, showing her the small coins.

At the fountain, they were nearly thrown off their feet by the surging crowds. Anne stumbled and was saved from a soaking only by the quick thinking of Emma who was concentrating hard on her task. She grasped her toppling mother just in time and righted her, while holding on to the three *baiocchi* in her other hand.

Closing her eyes and turning around, she held the three coins in her right hand and tossed them over her shoulder. They landed with a tiny sprinkling splatter and the approval of several bold Italian youths who were standing by in an effort to woo the young ladies who were looking for love. Emma knew better than to heed their nonsense, and looked at her mother. "What do you suppose it means to have a new love?" she said, looking straight at her mother.

"I think it will give you what it gave me: a return to Rome, a new love, in your father, and a marriage."

Emma sighed, smiling. "I hope you are correct, mother," she said.

Turning away from the beautiful fountain with its cascades among the astonishing sculptures of Roman gods, Emma was intent on finding the Sistine Chapel. Grasping her mother's arm, she pulled her away from the fountain.

"We must get to the Sistine Chapel, and this guidebook shows us the way. We can cross the Tiber to get there."

"But Emma, it is miles and miles away. We must take a coach." But there were no coaches to be had in Rome at this time and so the two ladies doggedly trudged from one side of Rome to the other, in time to see the Sistine Chapel, and all the beautiful paintings on the ceiling. By the time they arrived, the chapel was getting ready to shut down for the evening prayers, and Anne had to beg them in Italian to stay open.

When they finally walked through these storied halls, they were stunned. Both of them expected something lovely, but neither of them expected something so sumptuous, something that would create stories in their minds.

"My goodness, mamma," said Emma with great enthusiasm. "The artwork in this chapel is beyond my imagination to conceive of. I daresay I shall never think of the Bible stories the same way again."

"What a fascinating perspective," she said, beaming at her daughter's piousness, mistaking it for what she assumed was a replacement for the young Italian nobleman.

"How do you mean?"

"Only that I am very impressed with your interest in the fine arts," said Anne.

Emma smiled. But in truth, both ladies were staggered by the scope of the work, by the sheer detail and variety of this masterpiece.

They did manage to secure a hackney to take them back to the *pensione*, and almost as soon as Emma had entered, Nell, who was still as unable to contain her emotions as ever, presented her with an envelope.

"It's from the Eye-talian gentleman," she whispered excitedly.

"I'll ask you to hold your tongue please, Nell," hissed Emma, in terror that her mother would hear. She slipped the letter into her breast to hide it from her mother and stole away to her room, where she opened and devoured it.

> "My dearest Emma: I wrote this same letter out seven times because I did not know where to find you. I want you to know that I will be writing to you at your England home, when you instruct

me to do so. This is the only thing that is holding me back. I await your orders and when I receive them, not only the letters will begin to litter your mail slot, but my very presence will grace your front door. For I cannot contain myself anymore, now that propriety no longer demands my physical temperance.

Now, freed from their earthly moorings, my thoughts will fly to you, with passion like a sun ray. And they have a question that must be answered, one that demands a response so that their bearer may live. Will you agree to be my bride? I will make this declaration if I know your love is true as mine is. I remain, your loving suitor,
        Federico Zane, Veneziano nobile."

The secrecy required to keep this news from her mother was daunting for Emma. As a young woman of irrefutable character, she had never kept secrets from her mother before, but having heard her mother's horror story, she had no desire to subject the dear lady to a revisiting of this awful story.

'But of course,' Emma told herself, 'this is a totally different situation. Federico is not a Lothario, nor was he trying to trick her; his love is true and he has gone out of his way to make this fantasy of ours a reality.'

And so, she decided to keep her most weighty secret from her mother, while sharing it with Nell. Nell was a cunning conspirator and a deft hand at procuring and dispatching missives to her lover. With her help, she managed to send three letters while they were in Rome, receive two, and forward their next known address, in Florence, a few days later.

They were travelling along one of the harshest roads in Italy, the road between Rome and Florence.

Sitting in the carriage, Anne, looking distinctly unwell, complained. "This is unbearable," she complained.

"Mother, it is only a test. We are on our way to see the most beautiful city in the entire world, and it is only natural that we must endure something. But, I am curious; why is this road so poor?"

"Madamina," said an elderly Italian gentleman who was overhearing their conversation. "Forgive me for intruding, but I can tell you exactly why it is such a poor road. You see, for many centuries the two cities were mortal enemies, and not allies as they are today. Many Popes in Rome would try to wage war on Firenze, and many of the Tuscan Dukes would wage war on the Roman states. And so, the roads have been made nearly impassable."

"That is fascinating, sir," said Emma. "But why do they not repair them now?"

"Brigands," said the Italian gentleman with a flourish.

Almost as though conjured up by this word, the carriage ground to a halt and there was the sound of voices raised outside. The gentleman looked out the window and shook his head. "It is happening again," he said. "This is the most lawless place in Italy!"

"What do you mean?" said Emma.

"I mean, we are being held up again."

"Again?"

"I am terribly sorry ladies, but it appears as though they are after your jewels."

"My jewels? I have no jewels."

"Well, these brigands are dangerous villains, and I suggest you do not argue with them."

"This is an outrage!" said Emma.

"Emma! Please be careful," said Anne, cowering in a corner of the carriage.

Emma though, emboldened by her newfound love, rose in her seat, and looked out the window. Although it was dark out and the coachman's lantern was swinging wildly in the wind, and so it was difficult to make out what was going on. She could see several men, the coachman and others, kneeling on the road, cowering in fear of their lives. Emma was a young woman who was not used to being disturbed and had strong ideas of her own about what was proper. She opened the door with a clang, and stood at the doorway.

"Just what on earth is going on?"

One of the brigands, holding a pistol in his hand, and wearing a kerchief over his face swung around in alarm. He shouted something in Italian that Emma did not understand.

"We are on our way to Florence. Andiamo!" she cried. "Get off the road!"

All of a sudden, there was the sound of a horse rearing up and clomping down again on the rough terrain. Somewhere in the darkness, there was a click of metal on metal, and Emma looked into the darkness, grasping the umbrella she had laid down. She pointed it at the source of the sound and said, "You are holding us up. Be on your way!" Another horse reared and some male voice was heard shouting, as they heard the horses gallop away.

There was a silence for a few seconds, and suddenly the driver leapt from the top of the coach on to the ground. He began to laugh. Then he turned to Emma and said in halting English. "My lady, you make these mens running away. So thankful am I for your work." He began to laugh, and Emma realized that she had frightened off some highwaymen. She sat on the edge of the carriage as she was surrounded by the gentlemen, none of whom was brave enough to do anything to help them.

"So, to be clear," Emma said, stunned. "That was a highwayman?"

"That was the feared Barbarossa, so named because of his tinted beard," said one of the English gentlemen. "He has captured and held many travelers in this region in his mountain lair. It is said that he tortures them and burns them at the stake if they do not pay his ransom."

Emma listened with skepticism. "But why would he run away when I brandished my umbrella?" she asked.

"The only thing Barbarossa fears is a woman with red hair," suggested one of the gentlemen.

"Really?" she said.

"Is true," said the driver. "He has been frightened by your hair. So red."

"I see," she said, and, in truth, she was rattled by her unintentional bravery. Emma took the lantern and walked off into the forest. The gentlemen dared not follow her, but stood together, frightened and somewhat humiliated. There was a rustling in the trees, and Emma could be heard calling out "Barbarossa! Barbarossa!" to the shame of the gentlemen.

After several minutes like this, the coachman took another lantern, plunging the travelers into darkness. He ran into the bushes and found Emma. "Please return to coach, Miss," he could be heard pleading with her.

Without a word, Emma returned. "Not a sign of the dread villain," she said, looking at the assembled gentlemen. "I must say, you are no gentlemen if you cannot save a weak and defenseless maiden such as I," she said in a mocking tone.

"you are no weak or defenseless woman," said the Englishman. Returning to the coach, she noticed that her mother was still asleep. Somehow, inexplicably, she had stayed asleep, while Nell, lantern eyed, was agog at the bravery and madness of her mistress.

"I never saw nothing like that in all me life!" she said. "And these gentlemen quaking in their boots. You are a mad woman but madam, I am devoted to you. You are braver than any person I have ever known!"

"Poppycock!" said Emma sharply. "That was no brigand. That was some silly prank and I have had enough of this. I am going to sleep!" And with that, she turned and went to sleep.

As soon as the coach arrived in Florence, the gentlemen who had been so free with their attention to Emma scampered off in search of some of their vanished pride, while Emma dismounted and alit on the pavement of the square in front of the church known as Santa Croce as though she had done nothing brave and with nary a thought in her head. She looked up at the lovely fifteenth-century architecture, seeing the world with new eyes. "Now this is living," she said, as she looked toward the tomb of Michelangelo Buonarroti, the sculptor of *David* that she had heard so much about. "I suspect this Michelangelo fellow made his own tomb then, did he?"

"No, madamina," said a guide who was standing near her. "This is the work of the great architect Giorgio Vasari. But is very beautiful, no?"

"It is very beautiful of course, but who would enjoy such a thing?" she asked. "A tomb is the least interesting thing I could ever imagine in which to live," she said tartly.

"Well, my dear, this is one of the wonders of Italy," said Anne, trailing behind her.

"I see," said Emma. "Then if all Italy has to offer me is a collection of handsomely carved rocks, I should like to return to England where the rocks are uncarved and the people are a little livelier."

"I shall endeavor to do your bidding," said Anne, a little sadly.

Nell, on the other hand, having been to the hotel and inquired about the post, was in a frenzy of emotion, trying her best to conduct herself in a seemly manner. "Emma!" she whispered. "There is a letter for you from the Eye-talian!"

Emma reached her hand out and grasped the letter, putting it in her bosom for safekeeping until she could read it alone.

"Mother, can we please return to the hotel and perhaps have a meal of some of that paste they serve here?"

"They call it pesto, daughter," said Anne with a grin. "And, of course you may. Let's us walk there now. I feel in need of a constitutional."

Although Nell had sent their bags on ahead, Emma was not able to convince her mother to take one of the hackneys that were circling the square, and so, together with Nell, the three of them strolled through the crowded Florentine streets back to their hotel. Once there, Emma flew to the dressing room, locking the door, and tore open the seal.

"My dearest darling," he began. "I am nearly broken in twain waiting to hear from you. My sleep is disrupted, and I cannot eat. I fear I am wasting away for want of your touch. I still remember the feel of your hand, as imprinted as it is on my palm, and I still remember your beautiful red hair, as strange to me as though you were from the moon. I have told my father that I will need to travel, and he has given me leave to visit England. I shall come with my valet, Guglielmo, who knows my every secret. I shall travel there in July. I trust you shall have returned by then. Do let me know by the next post if you have other plans, but I lay myself at your feet, and swoon with delight at the sight of your face again. I shall be there, and I shall have my request for you darling. I cannot wait for the chance to embrace you forever. I remain, your loving suitor, Federico Zane, Veneziano nobile."

It was the turn of the brave and stoic Emma Shaftesbury to swoon with passion. This man who was not even English had a way of writing to her that made him seem so close and so desperately wonderful. Her need to return was suddenly redoubled and she left the dressing room with resolve.

"Mother, we must return to England at once," she announced.

"But Emma, we have seen none of the wonders of Florence."

"I care nothing for them now nor ever," declared Emma. "I tell you I have had enough of these foreign climes and the weather that never seems to cool off. It is wearying and I need to be home where the rain comes to make things right. Oh, please mother, let me go!"

Flummoxed, Anne looked at her daughter with pity and desperation. She would do her bidding of course - she must! But how? She then looked to the ever-willing Nell.

"Nell, darling," she said with an oily tone. "Could you be so kind as to set a voyage by coach to return to our country?"

"Of course, ma'am," said Nell as she curtsied and left the room. Within the hour, Nell had somehow secured passage in a first-class carriage bound for Land's End, for three gentlewomen (she emphasized this, remembering her uncomfortable ride atop the carriage from Calais to Paris) on the morrow, at ten.

"Oh Nell, you have worked miracles for this entire journey. I think you deserve considerably more wages than you currently receive. What do you think?"

"I think I could always use a little more," said Nell, knowing that this idea would go straight out of her mistress' head the moment she saw England.

"Your abilities as a tour guide and arranger of the affairs of people who knew not how to help themselves is extraordinary, Nell," she said. "I daresay that when you come to live with me in my household, you shall be the butler, so indispensable you are."

Nell laughed heartily. "Ma'am," she said. "That is an honor I could not possibly undertake, for I doubt that you should like me to be present when your true love dresses himself."

Emma knit her brow. "Yes, that would be indecorous," she said. "But I shall reward you nonetheless, for I realized today that you are utterly indispensable."

"Thank ye, milady," said Nell with a curtsey and a mock-serious tone.

And the following morning their baggage was packed in a seemly manner and loaded onto the coach that arrived promptly at ten, and set off only a few minutes later with the three ladies and their baggage.

Emma set herself a comfortable nook in the corner of the carriage beside her long-suffering mother, and fell fast asleep. While the carriage rumbled through the pass uneventfully, Anne was very happy. They passed Bologna and Milan within seven hours, and the coachman, who seemed to be well prepared for any eventuality, put them all up in an inn on the outskirts of town. Anne and Emma slept on a bed of hay for the first time in their lives and awoke feeling strangely refreshed. The next morning, after a meal of egg-bread and coffee, they were again on their way.

The next stop would be Parma, passing Modena, and when they arrived in Parma, they had lunch of that same delicious pesto with some local cheese called Parmigiana. Feeling rejuvenated, they decided to continue on their way, and by nightfall, they had reached Milan.

Time had a way of blending together in these journeys like a clever blending of colors on a beautiful painting, and before they knew it, they were in Geneva. As the driver needed to tend to his horses, they were forced to spend a couple of days admiring the watches in the shops. Geneva was an orderly city and had always been an orderly city, and so Emma took Nell with her to sit in a coffee house and write a letter to Federico.

"Dearest, I pray you get this letter. I have been so bored lately that I am ready to scream. I am winging my way back to Canterbury so I can await your arrival. The little town of Geneva is so absolutely dull that I refused to raise my head as we drove through. Sadly, we were forced to stop and water the horses. I visited the shop of a little watchmaker and found a gentleman's watch that I bought to present to you when you arrive. I am most excited to show it you. Otherwise, all is living for the future. For our future, my love. By all accounts I may be home within the week and I trust you will be arriving not long afterward. I remain yours, truly, deeply, and forever, my angel, your Emma."

This was the first letter where she let herself go entirely and admit that she was madly in love. As she was. Back on the coach, she held the little watch she had purchased for Federico in her hand, turning it, imagining it on his waistcoat, and dreaming of the day where she could listen to the heartbeat of his love for her through the ticking of the watch.

It was only a matter of a few hours later, when they entered Lyon, and both Nell and Anne commented as to how much more comfortable this ride was. It was on a sprung coach, the driver told them, and this made all the difference.

In a few days, they were back in Paris, taking a day to rest.

"Miss Emma," said Nell. "We must go back to that little shop to look at the dresses."

"Yes we must," said Emma, rushing down the stairs, and into the street, forcing Nell to run after her. The two of them were in front of "Au Petit Dunkerque" within the hour.

"Dear God, ma'am, but that dress is still in the window!"

"That is wonderful," said Emma, transported by its perfection. She still remembered what it looked like on her slim form. She knew that if she were to own it, Federico would swoon at her feet the moment he saw her in it. But sadly, they were no wealthier on this return journey than they had been for the first trip and she knew better than to pester her mother who was laid up in the hotel room with a summer fever.

"Mother, I am very eager to get back to England. Is there any way at all that you could finish your malady while en route?" said a cheeky Emma, smiling at her mother, but still hoping that she would acquiesce.

"Emma, we shall go when I feel that I am able to travel."

"Well, I feel that the Paris air is bad for you. Perhaps if we traveled to Arras?"

"Emma, we can go the moment I feel up to traveling."

"Very well," said Emma, kissing her mother on the cheek affectionately.

And Anne was convinced too, in short order. Within a day, she had ordered a coach to take them to Arras to stay at the country inn where Emma had had a bath.

When they arrived, Emma looked at her mother with concern

"Mother, I want you to have a bath this time. I shan't abide you sniffling your way through this journey and if you don't do it I shall throw you in body and soul, so that you can return to yourself. You cannot tell me you may catch a chill for it is the height of summer."

"I dare say not, child!" said Anne. "It is the overheating that worries me. I have no desire to expose myself to that sort of filth."

"Mother, it is hot and you have been too hot, and we can ask the landlady, Madame de Mortier and her two servant girls to make a cool bath."

"Alright, my dear. You may ask them to do this, but I know the French and they will do it their way, and I shall catch my death."

However, Emma approached Mme. De Mortier ad spoke to her in French, explaining to her that her mother was overheated from travel and needed a cool bath.

"Of course we can do that!" said a friendly uncharacteristically friendly Madame de Mortier. And so, once again, she ascended the stairs laden with water for the bath and prepared this wondrous thing, this time for the lady of the family. And Madame de Mortier took Emma by the hand and led her to the lady's parlor and plied her with a *digestif* while Nell, who had grown very bold since her first time visiting Arras, helped Anne undress and prepare for the bath.

In the lady's parlor, there were several chatty French ladies who artfully ignored Emma. This sort of public censure put Emma in a mind to entertain, and so she purposefully stood up and went to the fortepiano that was by the window. She sat down at it and began to sing a song that she was very fond of, by the composer Muzio Clementi, who had written many songs in English. After a brief introduction that stunned the French ladies into silence, she began to sing:

> "Oh sing to me of your love gone wrong,
> Do not bring me your cakes and ale;
> For my heart cannot bear the pain

of the thought of my love gone stale."

The music was melodious and her voice pretty, but she played loud chords that disturbed their attempts at conversation. On she went, singing more and more verses in English. When she finished, several of the young French ladies gave a noticeable sigh and so Emma took this as encouragement. She sang an old Irish ditty called "She moved through the fair" which was as melancholy as anything she had ever heard, although the words echoed her feelings precisely:

> My young love said to me, "My mother won't mind
> And my father won't slight you for your lack of kind."
> Then she stepped away from me and this she did say:
> "It will not be long, love, till our wedding day."
>
> She stepped away from me and she moved thru' the fair
> And fondly I watched her move here

and move there.
And she made her way homeward with one star awake
As swan in the evening moves over the lake.

Last night, She came to me, She came softly in
So softly she came that her feet made no din,
And she laid her hand on me and this she did say:
"It will not be long, love, till our wedding day."

Her voice was beautiful and the lugubrious chords she played to accompany herself on this instrument were stirring her to tears. Her voice cracked several times to think of the possibility of her love. Slowly the French ladies, sensing the true sentiment in her singing began to listen and to heed her songful warnings.

And when she had finished, they clapped with their gloved hands, complimenting her on her voice and her choice of songs. Emma then spoke to them in French, and they were mightily impressed that she could speak to them, noting with a certain hauteur that the English were not eager to speak their language.

"I love languages myself," declared Emma, and told these ladies of the love she had found in Italy. Scandalized, the younger of the three turned to her and said, "Are you not afraid that your family will disown you? In France, if we marry out of our station we will lose our position in the family, our inheritance, whatever dowry we may have been promised, and our trousseau. It would be a catastrophe!"

"My dear," said Emma. "My mother fell in love with a Venetian many years ago and so she understands this situation. She does not yet know that I plan to marry a Venetian gentleman, but I shall win her over."

"And where is your mother now?" said the elder of the three, whom Emma took to be the mother. "For I can see that you are not the sort of lady who would go about unchaperoned."

"She is taking a bath," said Emma loudly, expecting a shocked gasp. However, when she said it there was no reaction at all. It was as though she said she was merely walking the high street. But the fact of the matter was that Emma felt a great freedom talking to these strangers without her mother hearing. She was most satisfied and when she finished her third aperitif, making the climb of the stairs to the third floor a trifle precarious, since the steps had become a great deal wobblier than when she had not had three aperitifs, she greeted her clean and happy mother with great emotion.

"Mother you look like a new woman," she said.

Nell, who was busy cleaning the mess made by Anne when she stepped out of the bath soaking wet, looked up at her. "Aye, and I'm an old woman," she said, wiping her brow like an Irish washerwoman.

"I must confess, although it is a terrible bother for the servants, this bath is formidable, as the French say. You were quite right when you said it would rejuvenate me. I feel as though I have washed ten years off my life."

With great ceremony, the door opened and Madame de Mortier entered with her two servants and took away the bath. Emma and Anne both thanked her with great enthusiasm, and both of them took to their beds promptly to be on the road early the next day, bound for Calais.

The trip across 'La Manche', as the French call the English Channel, was tortuous. Weather had agreed with them every day since they had been in Florence and it decided to save it all up for the channel crossing. They had boarded the ship with great ceremony, noting the gathering clouds on the horizon with trepidation. Emma heard an old salt declaring with great certainty that "she's due for a wild crossing," and kept this knowledge to herself, ensconcing her mother in a cabin down in the ship's belly.

"Have you noticed the change in the weather?" asked Emma.

"I am quite worried, to be honest, ma'am," said Nell, looking at the gathering clouds. "It looks like a storm is on the way."

No sooner had they cast off than she felt the air become thick and angry. The time was no more than three o'clock and yet it became dark as night and ominous.

Moving to the deck area, she noticed the tars were scampering around up and through the sails, like ants before a storm.

"Pardon me, sir, but what is the hurry?" asked Emma to one of the tars who was rushing by.

"No time to talk, Miss," he said. "Storm's a coming."

Before she had time to ask any of them what the rush was, the sea answered her. It rose up in a most dramatic way, tossing their ship like a cork. The waves that broke over the prow of the ship turned to mist by the time they were midship, and Emma enjoyed the beginnings of the storm as a misty morning on the heath. Within minutes though there were terrible billows rising and she was battered hither and yon, holding to the wooden sides for dear life.

    Nell had long since descended below, determined not to ruin her frock. But Emma wanted to face the anger of the sea gods and stayed where many of the sailors dared not go. There were times when she feared for her life but other times that she felt braver than the explorers who went ashore on the wild and savage lands they had discovered in the darkest regions of the earth. Her bravery in her mind was mixed with the folly that the captain perceived when he yelled through the gale at her to "get below for heaven's sake lest ye be washed over to Davy Jones locker!"

    Emma smiled at their worry, knowing that she had power in her soul that would save her regardless of the anger of the oceans and before several hours had passed, the storm too had passed, leaving a soaking but clean deck on which to tread, and a sodden Emma Shaftesbury feeling alive in a way she had not felt since the kiss from her Arlecchino all those months ago. Indeed, the fury of the force of the wind and the spray were invigorating to an Englishwoman in a way that they could not be for any other person. She made a note of this, to tell Federico the next letter she wrote. Before she could go below to write though the tar in the crow's nest hallooed "land ho!" and she had to prepare to take her bags off the ship. She went below where she found her mother feeling peakèd, and somewhat the worse for wear.

"Oh mother, you look positively dreadful. Whatever happened to the new woman you became after that bath?"

"I fear she was washed overboard," said Anne with a sly grin. She composed herself promptly and rose to oversee the unpacking of the baggage.

Nell, indispensable as ever, procured for them a coach that could bear them to their home in Canterbury. She found an idler in the pub at the harbor who was complaining about his lack of work.

"I say, my good man, if you desire work, I have a task for you that would be the envy of any coachman."

"And what be that, my wench?" he said in a coarse tone.

Nell, who had merely stepped into the public house to ask for help, was taken aback by his effrontery. "You may take two ladies of good family and standing and take them home after their journey to the continent."

"I does that every day of me life, missy," he said. "And what business is it of your'n, if I might ask?"

"My mistress and her mother are fatigued by a perilous journey from France, and having foiled a highwayman, and entranced half of Italy with their brilliance, they have but one desire, and that is to be taken hope in a warm coach, by a courteous coachman. Would ye know of one?" said the cheeky maid.

"Why I'm the best there be," he said, spilling ale onto his frock coat.

"You'd best be willing to prove yourself then, for I am prepared to engage you for a good rate."

The coachman wiped his lips dry and took the bait. "I stand ready and willing to ferry these lasses to their abode. Let us depart then, my cheeky wench."

Without a word to her mistresses, Nell came out of the public house followed by the burly coachman. "We will depart presently," she declared.

The mother and daughter were sitting on a bench, lost in their own thoughts when suddenly they looked at Nell. "Where have you been?" said Anne. "We've been beside ourselves."

"I have procured us transport home," she said flatly. "And so, let us follow this brute as he is our ferryman."

The two ladies followed without a word, both of them too worn out to protest. They sat in the coach in a semi-conscious state for the several hours' coach trip home. This coach was no match for the well sprung Italian coach, and its buck board suspension left them rattled by the time they pulled up in the courtyard of the manor. Nell, alert as always, had ridden up with the driver telling him where to go, and without fail, she had succeeded in making him do her bidding.

The very moment their coach rounded the bend and came into view of the manor, the butler, Simmons, was seen coming out the door. As the coach stopped at the door, Simmons reached up, opened the door and allowed the two ladies to leave the coach. Nell climbed down from the top of the coach and paid the driver. "You have done yeoman service, my good man," she said with conviction. The brute leapt down to the ground, grinning. "Thank ye kindly miss," he said, pocketing his pay.

Simmons discreetly passed a letter to Emma. "This missive arrived by yesterday's post, madam," he said with weight. Emma looked at the post mark, *Venezia*, and smiled. "I shall read it the moment we are in the house," she said, putting it in her breast.

Inside, while the bags were being removed from atop the carriage, she tore open the letter.

> "Dearest Emma," it read. "I depart today for your clouded island. I cannot wait any longer, and I will bear with me a very important decision. Please write to me in Paris, where I shall wait for your permission to attend to you in the manor. I am consumed with the fires of affection, and dare not wait any longer. I shall be there within the week, once I receive your letter. My address is contained in the calling card that is contained in this envelope. I await your response with baited breath. Yours ever and always,

Federico Zane, Veneziano nobile."

Emma held the letter to her breast, breathing with difficulty as though she had climbed a high hill. She was lightheaded and stunned by this sudden escalation of their amour. She flew to her desk and began to write furiously.

"My darling Zane: I urge you to come with all speed. I fear my family will try to marry me off to the wealthiest fop in the kingdom and if you are not here to defend my honor, I fear the worst. Do fly to me, and claim me as your own, for I am ever and always your own Emma."

She folded and stuffed it into an envelope. She found the small card, noting that it was the hotel on the Champs Elysée, and hastily scribbled a post script. "Dear Federico, if you pass by a shop on the Champs Elysée called "Au Petit Dunkerque," please look at the beautiful dress and buy it as I would like this to be my wedding dress!" Having daubed the wet ink with her blotter, she again put the letter into the envelope and ran to Simmons, begging him to post it with all speed.

Chapter 10. The Lost Dress

Emma spent the next few days in a state of emotional turmoil. Her love for Federico grew as though tended by a very eager and careful gardener; at the same time, her mother Anne, wanting to avoid any unpleasantness, took to her writing desk, writing letters aplenty, inviting all the eligible bachelors in the area to a ball to be held in honor of the triumphant return of her daughter Emma.

"Mother, I really wish there to be no fuss about my return. Perhaps Lizzie has a new beau. Could we not focus on this issue at present? I have no desire to meet an eligible bachelor."

"Emma, my dear, you are new to this world and I urge you to take my advice. The iron is hot at the moment and there are many young men in search of a bride. You are now the most eligible lady in the country, and I propose for you to marry well in order that you may begin your life as an adult. Consequently, I have arranged for a wonderful affair in our own drawing room. We have engaged the finest orchestra in the area to lead the dance and I assure you it will be a fruitful endeavor."

Emma, unable to tell her mother the news of Federico's imminent arrival, had to bow to her urgings. "Alright mother, but I do wish we had bought that frock in Paris. I was most enamored of it. I declare I would marry the man who managed to acquire it for me."

"Darling daughter, you must give up these fancies, for that dress is surely already gone. Concentrate on the serious issue of marriage, for it is not to be entered into lightly."

And with that, she swept out of the dining room, to oversee the preparations for the dance.

It was a mere two days later that the ball took place. The orchestra was installed at the far end of the long drawing room, and refreshments were set up on the dining table. The ball was set to commence at seven o'clock sharp and guests were to arrive at six in order to mingle. Emma herself was dressed and ready to go at five, desiring more than anything that her Venetian suitor would arrive and sweep the rabble from her door. And yet she dared not hope that he had received the missive in time to prevent the suitors' ardor. Elizabeth, Emma's younger sister, with whom she had shared nearly everything, came into her room without knocking, startling Emma who was dressed and staring into her dressing mirror.

"Emma, this charade simply cannot continue," said Elizabeth with a maturity beyond her years. "But I've seen to it that no young man will be alone with you. I have instructed the orchestra to play a longways country dance, a Scotch reel, and a Cotillion before the break. None of your continental intrusions. None of those waltzes that you spoke of in Venice, and no opportunity for a suitor to pull you aside and declare his undying love."

"Oh Elizabeth, you are such a dear. I am absolutely devoted to you."

"And I ask only that you be discreet should you see something which may strike you as unseemly taking place between my person and a certain young man who shall remain nameless," she said slyly.

"I think you owe me a trifle more information than that!" said Emma, turning from the mirror and looking a flushed Elizabeth square in the face.

"Very well," said Elizabeth. "Are you familiar with a man with a certain large income, perhaps three thousand a year, who has been making a mockery of convention in this part of the country of late?"

Emma was speechless, hearing this sort of chatter coming from her sister, who had been a child when she left and was clearly an adult now. She was only just eighteen and thus of marriageable age, but had not as yet been brought to the Capital, and she not been brought out. Nevertheless, Emma listened with rapt attention to her secret.

"No, of course you haven't. You see, he seems to have sprung fully formed from the head of Zeus, as our governess likes to say. His name is D'Arcy Hamilton, and he has recently returned from the Continent where he was touring. He is positively dashing and he has lately declared his love for me. He was invited by mama, unwittingly, and I shall find some time to spend with him, as long as I have your word of honor that you will not say a word." Emma was stunned into silence.

Chapter 11. The Grand Ball

As is the wont of parents eager to marry off their daughters to a good family, in order to ensure her future happiness, the continued wealth of the family lineage, and to enrich themselves a trifle, Emma Shaftesbury's parents spared no expense for the ball they held in their drawing room. Emma cared not a fig.

It should be mentioned that when one thinks of a drawing room, one generally pictures a room that would hold about twenty people comfortably, in a civilized conversation. This would be a mistake when speaking of the drawing room in Godington Manor however, since this drawing room was a close second to St. Mark's Square, the "greatest drawing room in Europe", as this room was very large and very well-appointed with all the necessary furniture to host a soirée such as this ball.

It was a warm July day and Anne had arranged for a particularly lovely frock to be created for Emma, with a conical skirt that looked very modish, and puffed sleeves and a deeply low neckline that revealed more than Emma thought was proper. Her mother though, was entranced by the effect this had made, and complimented the appearance of the lilac silk material on her shapely daughter.

"Mother, this is scandalous!" said Emma. "You know I am modest of my bosom! This is tantamount to advertising in the most crass and indiscreet manner of Fleet Street!"

"My darling daughter," began Anne, and Emma knew that this meant she was planning something frightening to her very soul. "You are the most eligible lady in the entire country. You have made the Grand Tour, you are beautiful and you are very much unspoken for. This ball will be the great unveiling of the lady most likely to marry in the next year. Therefore, you must look the part, and to accentuate your strengths is no small way to ensuring both your future happiness and security, but also the family's fortunes. It is no secret that your father has enriched our family and this knowledge along with your very lovely qualities will make the young men who have been invited to this ball very eager to make your acquaintance."

"Mother, they all know me, and they also know that they are of no interest to me."

"No interest to you? How can this be? Who on earth do you expect to attract with an attitude of boredom?"

"I have my preferences mother, and none of these silly boors is of any interest to me."

"Will you please give them a chance? I fear you have underestimated their geniality and goodwill. Do us all a kindness and please go to this ball with an open mind and an open heart. If not for your own happiness, do it for the safety of your mother and your family name."

"Very well, mother. I shall go to this silly ball and do my best to woo some fop."

"Do not call these young men fops. It is very rude." Her mother looked askance at her daughter, but finally decided to trust that her daughter would not continue to be headstrong and self-destructive when she saw the gentlemen she had handpicked to woo her. Perhaps it was true that they would not all be gems, but some of them were very well-off, with incomes of upwards of five thousand a year. She descended the grand staircase and made her entrance to the joy of the elder invitees.

At eight o'clock, long after all the gentlemen had arrived, and all the ladies had shared several dances with these men, Emma made her entrance. She was breathtaking in her new gown and the little purple slippers that peeked out from beneath her lilac frock. Her wild mane of red hair was pulled up into a fetching bun, and its pearl clips glinted in the lights of the chandeliers that dotted the ceiling of the drawing room.

She had chosen an opportune time to enter, just as one dance had finished and before the next had begun. Slowly but surely, all eyes turned to her and she knew she was making an impression, despite her deep desire not to do so.

Thomas Parker, son of one of the wealthier landowners in the district, was first to approach her. He wore breeches in the old style, with white hose, and black dancing shoes, and a waistcoat. His hair was a trifle longer than it had been the last time she saw him and his mutton chops had grown in, making him quite manly-looking. At least it might have looked this way to a lady who had just met him and not one who had known him since childhood, where his pink complexion belied his twenty-three years.

The withering look on Emma's face made Thomas Parker turn his stride toward the young Misses Charlotte and Emilia Marlowe, who were watching Emma by the punch bowl, and entirely unaware of his approach. Emma watched him try to strike up a conversation with them and would have been amused were it not for the approach of another potential suitor, John Merriweather, whose father was a peer of the realm and the Earl of Doncaster. John was his eldest son, and as such would stand to inherit both the title and the considerable wealth. He was upon Emma before she could rebuff him.

"The weather is unseasonably warm," he said, and Emma noticed a bead of sweat tracing its way down the side of his face. She could tell he was nervous, and somewhat tongue-tied, for it was July and the weather in July was predictably balmy.

"Yes, but it will snow tomorrow, you can count on it," said Emma with mock seriousness. The poor stupid heir knew not what to say and so he wisely held his tongue. "John Merriweather, are you going to ask me to dance?" asked Emma coquettishly. John was so shy that he was unable to respond other than by coloring a distinct red in his cheeks. But the smile that broke out on his face belied his enthusiasm.

He stepped backwards, treading on Miss Emily Bracebridge's slipper. She cried out, unaware of what was happening, and the poor John Merriweather turned on his heel in shock and hit her arm, splashing her punch on her décolleté. This mad and inappropriate indiscretion, accidental though it was, would cause him to be dubbed "John the Baptist" by Emma.

For the next hour, she swanned around, refusing dances from prospective suitors, and telling the tale of John the Baptist, who had christened Miss Bracebridge with her own punch. She was the toast of the witty set, a small clique of outspoken single women who congregated around Emma, finding in her a voice they lacked, but envied.

Dance after dance began and ended without Emma stepping foot on the dancefloor. Time seemed to pass agonizingly slowly for Anne and Rufus Shaftesbury, who were overseeing this affair.

Elizabeth Shaftesbury, on the other hand, who had made her entrance even later than Emma, dressed in a light-yellow dress with an ample bosom and pretty embroidery around the hem, was making more of an impression on the young lads who were supposed to be interested in Emma. She was conversing with great glee with many of these young men, who had turned their backs on Emma, for fear that she would find a sobriquet for them too.

 All young men of this age, regardless of how confident they may appear, have chinks in their armor, and mockery by a young woman of marriageable age is the most gaping hole in their confidence. Consequently, many of them avoided Emma's acid tongue, and were drawn to pretty young Elizabeth with her tawny complexion and ash blonde hair, her pretty nose and her twinkling eyes.

 Sadly for them, though, D'Arcy Hamilton had entered unseen by Elizabeth or Emma, and while all the other young ladies turned away from their dandies to look at the figure he cut there in the golden candlelight - a dashing gallant in a beautiful London fashion and top hat, Sir D'Arcy had eyes only for young Elizabeth. This predicament was not lost on Anne and Rufus Shaftesbury who had hoped Sir D'Arcy, with his lands and his money, would be wooing their eldest daughter. Although he was a well-known cad, if one can trust the rumors that had been swirling since his return to society after graduating from Oxford, having ruined more than one housemaid, and jilted two young ladies in the west country, he was still a very attractive match for Emma. Emma, though, cared nothing for any of these Englishmen; she, too, had been ruined by her Italian suitor, whose ardor was evident even on the written page.

And suddenly the doors, which had been closed to visitors, were opened with great ceremony. All eyes turned to the double doors which had been closed only a few minutes after the appearance of Emma Shaftesbury. She was to be the last person at the ball, and so this indiscretion was seen by all as a terrible faux-pas on the part of the servants.

Nell came charging through the doors, looking around desperately for Emma, by the punchbowl, surrounded by the single ladies who were laughing uproariously at Emma's "bon mot" about the now-humiliated John Merriweather, who had slunk off to a corner to nurse his invisible wounds inflicted by the acid tongue of Emma.

"Miss Shaftesbury, we have a most untoward eventuality," said Nell with an attempt at erudition, trying to emphasize the strangeness of her appearance.

"What is it?" said Emma, suddenly deeply concerned for her maid.

"There's a gentleman who requests entry," she said, her eyes saucers of terror.

"A gentleman has appeared at this hour?" said Emma, knowing it was past ten.

"Not just any gentleman, Miss Shaftesbury; it's your Eye-talian gentleman."

The words hit Emma at her core. Federico had arrived. And at such an inopportune time. Propriety would dictate that he not be admitted, and all the young ladies began to titter about this most improper turn of events.

"Admit him," said Emma, looking around at the young ladies, who were struck dumb by this further impropriety.

"But Miss," protested Nell. "We were instructed to -"

"Admit him!" she repeated with ardor. "I will not have a gentleman who has ridden here from Italy go home without at least a little refreshment. Admit him at once!" She looked to her parents who were looking confused and bewildered. Nell, for her part, receded into the entrance, and moments later, appeared with a calling card in her hand. She stood in the entrance, and the music stopped, the orchestra sensing that something untoward was transpiring.

In the silence, Nell cleared her throat, and studied the calling card, which, in the Italian tradition was bordered with black.

"Signore Federico Zane, Veneziano nobile," she said with a very good pronunciation.

The whole room went deathly silent as the young man appeared, his long hair brilliantly coiffed, his flowered mustache heavily waxed. He made a tall and elegant figure dressed in a stunning Italian suit. He wore tight black trousers with a broad stripe down the side, a tight-fitting red serge waistcoat over a beautifully tailored shirt with ruffles at the wrists and the throat. He looked entirely unlike any of the dandies at the ball.

His flowery moustache and his bright black eyes, his Roman nose and his full red lips, opened to reveal a set of perfectly straight white teeth, drawing a gasp from the assembled ladies. Emma's heart flew out of her body and she felt as though she would swoon.

She grasped on to a chair back, and smiled broadly at his elegant appearance. Her eyebrows rose almost to her hairline and a smile broke out on her face along with an audible gasp of joy.

For a moment, Federico stood, leaning on a walking stick, one leg bent and the other straight like a military bow. There was a long silence during which John Merriweather was heard to stumble over a carpet. Then, looking around the room, surveying the assembled gentry, Federico saw Emma and turned to one side, as though he were firing a pistol at the gentlemen congregated together by the orchestra. Emma began to run toward him in a moment that seemed to slow the very orbit of the earth, her gown shimmering in the candlelight, and she met him only steps from open doorway, embracing him in an overt display of affection.

"My God, Federico!" she said with great joy. "You came!"

"Was there any doubt?" he asked in nearly unaccented English.

"I never doubted that you would come, but not so quickly!" she said, embracing him the closer.

The Shaftesbury père and mère were perturbed and began to move to calm the room. Both of them ceremoniously walked toward the couple, with an expression that none who were there could have known. Steps away from the couple, they both stopped. Anne turned to her husband and declared in a loud and clear voice, "Sir Rufus Shaftesbury, may I present Federico Zane, the son of a noble Venetian family."

Sir Rufus had no idea how to greet a noble Venetian, any more than he would have known how to greet a visitor from the moon. He looked uncomfortable in the way only a noble Englishman can, his right eyebrow raised, his mouth agape, and his feet far apart. He extended his hand tentatively, and Federico, his wits fully about him, grasped it and shook it forcefully.

"Pardon my intrusion, my Lord," he said. "I have travelled many miles for this honor. I apologize if I have come at an inopportune moment. It would appear that you are in the midst of a grand ball."

"Quite, quite," he said. "Well, I say, that is, well, of course we are having a little soirée, but an honored guest such as yourself is always very welcome. I am at a disadvantage though, you see, for I do not believe our families know each other."

"I believe, my dear, that you recall my Grand Tour before my marriage to you," said Anne.

"Why, yes, of course."

"The Zane family are one of the most distinguished in all of Venice," said Anne. "I lodged with them in my youth, and we visited them in Venice. Young Federico's father Michele is a friend of my family, and his son Federico is a most accomplished young man with a considerable fortune."

"Indeed?" said Sir Rufus with interest. "But, of course, I am most impressed. Tell me, Signore Zane, what is your business at the Godington Manor."

"My business, Sir Rufus, if I may be permitted, is to ask your daughter's hand in marriage." A gasp went through the room at this, for Federico was given to a certain theatrical bent. He spoke louder than most English, and his voice had a very theatrical ring to it. He could be heard even as far as John Merriweather's ignoble corner, and he could be heard to drop a glass. The tinkling of the shattered glass gave the punctuation to the sentence.

"Emma?" said a bewildered Sir Rufus.

"I ask your permission," said Federico. "I bring with me a considerable fortune, and I am willing to move to England and purchase a manor not far from here. I have the means the desire to do anything and everything that is required to secure your blessing, sir."

"I see," said Sir Rufus. "This is a most unexpected pleasure, of course, and I shall need a moment or two.... nay, a week, let us say, to come to a decision. Understand, young man, that a marriage is a sacred bond that is inseparable by neither man nor woman, and as such must be entered into with the greatest of care. Therefore, that is, I shall need a week!"

"Very well," said Federico, with great civility. "I bow to your power and your wisdom. For I must say that I entered into this love-bond with more ardor than planning. I love Emma with all my heart and will provide for her anything her heart desires. I do hope that you will agree to this proposal."

"Oh father!" cried Emma suddenly, tears staining her cheek. "I do so love Federico, and I would be heartbroken if you should deny us our happiness."

"Emma, I would ask you to stay out of this, if you please," said Sir Rufus. "This is a decision that, while I desire your agreement, is to be decided with a cold eye and a stern demeanor. I shall need a week. Good day." And with that, Sir Rufus bowed and turned to leave.

Anne looked at Emma, a broad smile on her face. If one were to enter into the mind of this brave woman, one would be able to see that she had once been faced with a not dissimilar situation, and that she had chosen Sir Rufus because of her fear of the unknown. Venice, at the time, was under the iron fist of Napoleon, the terror of all Europe, and a mortal enemy to the English. She wanted to marry Michele but was terrified unto death of the possibilities of danger and uncertainty. Consequently, she married the noble and moneyed Sir Rufus Shaftesbury rather than the precariously situated Michele Zane. In some magnificent turn of fortune's wheel, she now saw in her daughter, the dearest thing in her life, a chance to right her greatest regret. However, to the casual observer, Anne appeared to follow her husband and his desires. Ever a dutiful wife, she went with him to their chambers and told him the story as much as she knew.

Emma, for her part, took a great interest in making sure that everyone knew who Federico Zane was. With great ceremony, she took him around to the gentlemen assembled, introduced him in great detail, impressing everyone around, with her memory. Even poor John Merriweather, the unfortunate victim of her barbed attack earlier in the evening, was introduced with great dignity. He managed to pull himself together enough to respond politely to the introduction, feeling somewhat that she had forgiven him for his stupidity and clumsiness.

The last gentleman to be introduced was the rake, D'Arcy Hamilton, who was standing, talking closely with Elizabeth. Although Emma did not approve of him on principle, she introduced the two men with dignity and decorum.

"I have been to Venice, my dear boy," said D'Arcy with what Emma heard as condescension. "The marvels of your little town are without number. I am a great admirer of your painter Tintoretto, whose wit and skill exemplify the Venetian genius. Wouldn't you agree?"

"Tintoretto is a very brilliant painter, but my dear sir, have you seen the work of

Veronese? For his work is more beautiful and wittier by far. If you have had the good fortune, as I have, of gazing upon his 'Feast in the House of Levi,' you will know the brilliance of the greatest of my Venetian compatriots."

"I know of his work but never had the chance to see it," said D'Arcy, with evident respect. He was proud to display his knowledge of the arts, and eager to learn more. It seemed that D'Arcy and Federico would become fast friends. This was what Emma wanted more than anything. Federico was an unknown quantity, and despite the fantastical impression he had made on the assembled Englishman, he was still an outsider. Any connection to the gentry would help his cause, and hers.

Elizabeth, her sister, was smiling ear to ear, watching this colloquy, hoping, no doubt, to impress her sister with her choice of beau. She was clearly smitten, and Sir D'Arcy seemed to be smitten as well. Cupid's arrow appeared not to have missed his mark this evening on several counts.

Before long, the orchestra began to play a familiar melody. Federico's ears pricked up and he smiled broadly. "La Valse!" he said, leading Emma to the dance floor. "Will you do me the honor?" he inquired.

"I would be delighted!" she said. The empty dance floor was suddenly their stage, and this scandalous continental dance that involved what most Englishmen would have considered a frightful closeness, began. They were the only two on the dance floor and all the assembled gentry looked upon this confident foreigner with envy.

He moved with a grace that was almost unbelievable. He was smooth yet manly, and Emma seemed to melt into his arms. She was, in fact, transported both by the music and by her memory of dancing with Federico was 'Arlecchino' in St. Mark's Square all those months ago.

Seeing this romantic and impressive sight, Sir D'Arcy took Elizabeth's hand and led her to the dance floor. She was blushing with pride and joy as he took her hand and clasped it to his bosom. The smile on her face lit up the room as she looked to Emma who, too, was clearly filled with love and joy at this unexpected miracle. For truth to tell, she had composed her letters with great care and great emotion, never truly expecting the reality to happen.

And the fact that it had transpired at the very moment when she was most dreading, showed that her faith on God's ultimate goodness was fulfilled. The two sisters and their beaux danced around the dance floor in circles of grace, and the admiration of the crowded gentry was palpable. None though, dared to compete with the performers, preferring to remain spectators to the greatest event that had happened in Kent in years.

The evening ended before one in the morning, and Emma looked at Federico. "Where are you lodging?" she asked.

"There is an inn not far from here, and I have a comfortable, if small, room, which I am forced to share with my valet. I shall stay there until your father has reached his decision. I have a card with the address. Do write to me as soon as you can. I forgot to present your father with my card, and so he may be wondering who I am. I trust you can convince him of my sincerity."

"Oh Federico," said Emma. "I will try with all my heart!" And with that, she presented Federico with the Swiss watch she had purchased in Geneva. "Please take this and know that the time moves more slowly when I am away from you."

"I shall treasure it always," he said, deeply moved.

"I say there, Signore Zane," cried Sir D'Arcy Hamilton. "Did I hear you say you were staying at the *Baying Hounds Inn*?"

"I do not recall the name," began Federico.

"Why it's the one just a mile down the road. I am staying there too. Come and ride with me!" His carriage was already trundling up as he opened the door with great ceremony, much to the joy of Emma who was quickly coming to love this suitor to her sister for his great intelligence and craft.

"I rode here on my horse, but I would gladly accept a coach ride," he said. "That way, you see, I shall have an excuse to return. I must needs fetch my horse in the daylight."

"Come! We must be on our way," said Sir D'Arcy, as Federico kissed Emma's hand and bid her adieu. He climbed into the coach and, as they drove off, Emma could see him and Sir D'Arcy conversing amiably.

She turned to Elizabeth. "I am greatly impressed with your suitor," said she.

"Is he not a delight? He is terribly wealthy I'm told," said Elizabeth. "And he's ever so dashing. Not like your foreigner, but for an Englishman he is remarkable, don't you think?"

"I trust he will be of great utility in our future plans, my dear sister," said Emma as

Lisa Brooks

they turned back to the manor, still lit up with a thousand candles.

Chapter 12. After the Ball

After Federico Zane left Godington Manor with D'Arcy Hamilton, Emma and Elizabeth retraced their steps to the manor, and Elizabeth accompanied her sister on her way to her bedchamber, eager to learn more about this Italian who had so surprisingly proposed in public at a ball designed to have her find a husband. To Elizabeth, the irony was rich.

"Oh Emma, I am simply struck dumb!" said Elizabeth.

"Lizzie, darling, you are not struck dumb and you never will be!" responded Emma, laughing at her sister's choice of words. "But I tell you, this man is to be mine."

"Emma, how delicious!" said Elizabeth. "But how in heaven's name are you going to convince father to let you marry this heathen?"

Emma was slightly annoyed for several reasons, one of them being the simple fact that she was a notorious talker, and the other being that Lizzie could possibly be struck dumb was as impossible to her as Nell forgetting something. It simply could never happen. She was also unused to being badgered about her choice of mate, and since this was the first man she had chosen for herself, she did not really want to discuss the plan to marry him with her sister who was known for telling everyone ever one of her deepest personal thoughts. But the truth was also that she was bursting with joy and could not contain herself much longer.

"It is not up to me to convince father," she said. "I believe with all my heart that Federico will be able to do that when he returns. You must admit he cuts a dashing figure!"

"He is charming … for a foreigner," said Elizabeth rather disdainfully. "Of course, I prefer the home-grown version of the charmer. Which is why I have decided that I shall marry D'Arcy Hamilton."

Emma, who was planning on talking more about Federico Zane, suddenly stopped and looked at Lizzie. "You have decided that you shall marry him, have you?" she said amused.

Lizzie was outraged. "And why shouldn't I? He is a most handsome man, wealthy, and well-positioned. He has upwards of three thousand a year, I know, although I confess I have no idea what that really means, except that it means that I shall never be hungry."

"It is a good income, but that is not the issue. The issue is that he is more than ten years your senior, and an inappropriate match."

"Nonsense!" said Lizzie with annoyance. "Men are supposed to be older than their spouses. It's only right." She paused, trying to think of another reason. "It's God's will!" she finally said, causing Emma to burst out laughing.

"God's will that you should marry that man who is clearly aligned with the devil? Pishtosh!" And she ran ahead of Lizzie into her bedroom and threw herself on the bed, rapt with joy about her future. Lizzie ran behind her, enraged but still filled with joy about the excitement and her newfound love of D'Arcy Hamilton. It is safe to say that her emotions were heightened in almost every way and she felt giddy and light-headed about the possibilities in the future for her. But she leapt on top of Emma anyway, tickling her and making her turn to defend herself.

"Get off me!" cried Emma, tossing her petite sister away, laughing. Then, apropos of nothing, she said: "he is not a heathen! He is a Roman Catholic!"

The following morning, she was awoken by a stirring in the lower floor. Flying to the door, Emma listened to the sound of her beloved's voice in the main hall.

"I have come to retrieve my horse," he said with great ceremony. "And, if the master of the house is available, I should like to have a conference with him." There was a silence for a minute, followed by a rush up the stairs by the Butler, Simmons, charging up the stairs to the master bedroom. A knock at the master bedroom door was greeted by the door opening and a hushed conversation, followed by "Confound him! I told him I needed a week to decide!" And then a pause. "Very well! Tell the lad I shall be down presently."

Emma was giddy with the possibility of life-long joy with her beloved. But given her position in the family, she knew that she would have to wait. And waiting for something this momentous was excruciating.

She called Nell to her and begged her to help with her dress. She chose a particularly lovely frock of light blue, with beautiful detail around the hem, in gold. She had Nell do her upswept coiffure so that she looked as beautiful as she possibly could and then she sat at her dressing table, nervously fingering the combs, and cleaning off the stray hairs that had collected on them. Within minutes, they were all cleaned off and her busy and nervous fingers could do nothing more.

She thumbed through her novel, the one by Fanny Burney called *The Wanderer*, and imagined her life with Federico as a wanderer, discovering the mysteries of the world. Perhaps, she contemplated, she could go to the New World and see the wonders of New York City, which had been much in the news of late.

"I must gather my wits," she thought to herself. "This is of the utmost importance. I cannot appear a fool before my father. He needs to know my serious intentions."

As she was thinking these thoughts, there was a knock at her chamber door. She looked at Nell who was pacing nervously. "Do get the door please, Nell," she begged, and Nell ran to the door and opened it on to Sir Rufus, dressed elegantly.

"I must speak with Emma," he said nervously. Nell admitted him, and he entered ceremoniously.

"Emma, are you as smitten with this Italian gentleman as he seems to be with you," he asked.

"Oh father, I am head over heels in love!" she said, immediately regretting her exuberance. "I mean, I am of course cognizant of the changes that would be necessary. Nevertheless, there truly is nothing I would like better than to be united with Federico. He is well-off and very good to me. I feel he would be a good husband."

"I understand," he said sadly. Perhaps he was regretful that she would be leaving the home. Perhaps he was just a little put off by the swagger of the young Venetian. But he nodded knowingly, and bade her adieu.

She heard him descend the staircase and enter into his private library with Federico. It took only a few short minutes and he came back out, and ordered the family to collect in the drawing room.

"I have come to a decision regarding Emma and this young Venetian, Federico Zane. He wishes to wed her, and I have given my blessing on the union. And as such, I will offer a wedding and a dowry of ten thousand guineas for this blessed union. Do any of you have an objection?"

Emma noticed that Federico was not there.

"Where is Federico?" she asked.

"He is awaiting my final response, which will be decided as a family," he said.

"I would be willing," said Anne, a trifle wistfully.

"I too," said Elizabeth.

All eyes were on Sebastian, the dull-witted twelve-year-old. "I don't like Italians," he said stupidly.

"Does this mean you do not give your blessing?" asked Sir Rufus, as if it mattered. He was always fair-minded and respectful of this process. Sebastian, unaccustomed to being the center of attention, blushed and shifted from foot to foot.

"Well, no. I suppose if Emma wants to become an Italian, I don't care, but I shan't be visiting her there."

"Very well, then," said Sir Rufus, looking at Nell. "Please bring the young man within." And Nell left quickly, re-entering moments later with Federico on her tail.

"We have reached our decision," said Sir Rufus. "We, as a family, would like to invite you into our fold. You have our blessing." The joy spread on to Federico's face as he slowly came to an understanding that he would be permitted to marry the eldest Shaftesbury girl.

"I am overjoyed," he said, laughing. And then he stopped. He knit his brow. "I would, of course, need to return to Venice and seek permission from my family, my father," he added.

"Well, naturally," said Sir Rufus as though this were simply a matter of a rubber stamp. Federico turned to Emma. "I am most honored to have you as a bride, and I will depart immediately for the continent."

"May we have a few moments alone, papa?" asked Emma.

"Naturally," said Sir Rufus, ushering the remainder of the family from the drawing room.

Alone in the room, Emma was weeping with joy. "I never dreamt this would happen, Federico," she said. "My joy cannot be measured."

"Nor mine," said Federico. "Is there anything your heart desires as a token of my pledge?"

"I would love something to remind me of you. A lock of your hair?" she suggested. Federico looked at her with some alarm as though he did not understand.

"It is a traditional memento in England," she said hesitantly, not really knowing if this were the truth, but knowing he would not know.

"Very well," he said. He looked at the table before them, noting a beautiful pair of mother-of-pearl inlaid scissors. He turned slightly to the side, as was his custom, and deftly cut a dark ringleted curl from his hair, handing it to her.

"I have a dream too, Federico" she said. "I should like to married in a dress I saw in Paris."

"I shall go and purchase it!" he promised. "Where did you see it?"

"It is in a small shop on the Champs Elysée called 'Au Petit Dunkerque'. It is a golden dress that is the most beautiful thing I have ever seen. I saw it only a few days ago there, in the window."

"Your wish is my command," he said. "Your father wishes to celebrate this happy news with a grand dinner tonight and he will invite some of the local dignitaries to meet me. He wants me to buy a local manor house, of course, and settle here. Is that your wish?"

"I confess I haven't given it any thought at all," said Emma. "I was imagining us as world travelers."

"Oh, I hate travel," he said, confusing Emma.

"I see," she said trying not to appear crestfallen. "So where would you like to live?"

"It matters not to me. Here or Venice. It is your decision."

That evening, the dinner was served. It was a large feast featuring a delicious French onion soup and a roast beef, that traditional meal of the gentry. There were several trifles for dessert and a fine claret offered to drink. Federico sat beside Emma, commenting on the food, noting how simple English cookery was, and how he was unused to eating such heavy fare.

Emma took it all in stride, simply enjoying his presence. "I must leave on the morrow, in the morning," he said. "I shall fly to Venice with all speed and return to you for the wedding, which should be not more than three months hence." He then moved to her and embraced her with a stunning display of joy and love, affection and hope. "I truly love you, Emma. I never dreamed I should leave my motherland, but for you, I will do anything, go anywhere."

"And I love you too, my heart!" said Emma, swelling with emotion.

After the dinner, he checked his new pocket watch, took his horse, and raced across the countryside to his inn, where he packed, ready to return forthwith.

Chapter 13. Letters from Abroad

The following morning, Emma awoke a new woman. She was betrothed, and any woman who is not changed by this is cold, she told herself, to justify her giddiness. She knew not how to dress, or what to do all day, running from one room to another, playing on the fortepiano with all her might, in a vain attempt to calm herself. She dashed off several letters to Federico, filled with love and joy and anticipation of great happiness, but none of this helped her to calm down. She finally came to terms with the fact that she was giddy and would remain giddy until she received a letter from Federico.

And wait she did. Two days with the post arriving but without a letter from him. On the third day, she received a letter he had written while in Calais, expressing his uncontrollable joy.

"I am delirious with joy at the prospect of being united with you, dearest. I can hardly see the road before me, but I know I must fly to my home and impart the news to my family. I confess I have a little bit of apprehension as this is so untoward, but I am sure my family will be overjoyed when I tell them whom I have chosen."

Emma was taken with his handwriting which was exquisite, and his formidable use of the English language.

But days passed without a word. Emma continued to pen epistles to him without response, and day after day she eagerly awaited the post for news. She too was apprehensive about the big changes in her life, and decided that she would like to live close to her family if at all possible.

Her father had engaged an Italian tutor to teach them all how to communicate with "the Italian side of the family", as he began to call the Zanes. Emma did not know, but suspected that he had written to Federico's parents, in order to demonstrate his interest in the union, but he never said a word, of course, as this was not an area of interest to women, according to him.

From Turin, Federico wrote again to express his delirious joy at having his life settled, and in the letter, he expressed a desire to buy the now vacant manor not two miles from her house.

Emma rushed to her writing table to agree. She had seen this house when it was the home of the lady dowager duchess of Kent, now deceased these two years, and she was eager to offer this lofty place her woman's touch. She let her imagination go wild with new and tasteful wall coverings from Venice, and delightful carpets from the finest oriental merchants in London.

From day to day, she drew up plans for bed chambers, dining rooms, drawing rooms, sitting rooms, offices, and various other details that she imagined would be useful in the new home she was praying for. But after the letter from Turin, she ceased receiving these letters, causing her to become more and more melancholy.

"Emma, what is the cause of your gloom?" asked her mother Anne, one morning at breakfast. "It seems to me that all your dreams have come true and you will be the happiest girl in the world in only a few short months. How can you be so downhearted?"

"Oh mother, I am sure it is nothing. Only that I have not heard a word from Federico in weeks. He hasn't written since he was in Turin, and that cannot be good news."

"They say that no news is good news, but I can sympathize with your predicament," said Anne, her brows furrowed. "I wonder what the hold-up is."

"I do hope I didn't frighten him away, although I was writing about how we can spruce up the manor down the road. I have been so excited, mother, that I have decided how to furnish almost every room."

Anne laughed heartily. "That is fine, Emma, but do not get ahead of yourself. I have heard there have been a few people who have expressed an interest in that ramshackle old tomb. But never mind. I'm certain there is no shortage of fine, stately homes to purchase in this area."

Emma looked forward, sipped her tea, and frowned.

For weeks, nothing was heard from the young Venetian nobleman. None of the family knew what to do.

"It is curious," her father remarked, "how everything in our future is held by this fine gossamer thread which leads to the errant cavaliere from Venice."

He seemed as powerless as the rest of the family. From day to day, he grew increasingly worried, but never let Emma know of his concern. Whenever he greeted her, he would put on a happy face, and greet her warmly as though nothing was amiss.

But something was amiss, and everyone in the household, with the possible exception of the dull-witted Sebastian, was keenly aware of it. The power seemed to have been sucked out of the family and visitors were keenly aware of the pall that had descended on Godington Hall. As a result, he began to avoid visiting even on at home days.

It was Emma who first recognized the writing on the wall. One morning, she rose and dressed before descending the stairs to breakfast, with a heavy heart. Sitting on the night stand was a package with a return address of the Baying Hounds Inn. It was addressed to her. Emma opened it and retrieved the pocket watch she had bought for Federico. The note, from the innkeeper said only "found this in the room of your fellow. Thought you might need it."

Emma began to shake uncontrollably. She slowly went into the dining room and sat down. "I've come to the conclusion that the marriage promised me is not to be. And in view of this, I no longer consider myself to be betrothed to Federico Zane."

When Anne heard these words, she dropped her cup of tea, shattering the cup on the saucer, and, she later noted, breaking up the painting of the Grand Canal that was etched on to its side.

"Very well," she whispered, turning her face away from Emma to avoid have her see her tears.

Sir Rufus, who was of a similar emotional state, nodded his head. "I'm terribly sorry, Emma," he said. "You have my sympathy. It is a terrible thing for a young lady to be jilted. And this gentleman living in Venice makes it all the harder, I warrant, as I suppose it casts a pall on that lovely city."

Emma, who had reconciled herself to this situation, resolved to make the best of it and get back out into society.

"Mother," she said. "I want to re-enter society, and I shall do it with my head held high. I suppose there is no shame in admitting the inevitable."

Anne nodded, trying her best to keep the tears that had filled her eyes from overflowing down her cheeks.

Chapter 14. An Encounter on a Coach

Emma Shaftesbury returned to society, a trifle damaged, perhaps a little embarrassed, but still the resilient woman she always had been. When she returned to the Capital, she attended balls held by the Prince Regent, the many affairs involving her class, including the many dinners and recitals at the crystal palace, in the newly built park known as Regent's Park, in which carriages would trundle along the roads, while young couples strolled along the regal lawns.

Emma, finding herself more and more bored by society, awoke one morning with a desire to return to the countryside and tranquility of Kent.

"Mother, I simply cannot abide this search for another mate. I need to return home to rest and return my sensibilities to their former confidence."

"My dear, you have solved my problem," said Anne. "You see, Elizabeth has also asked to return, since her suitor will be in Kent in the next week. Could you accompany her on a coach? I shall be forever in your debt."

"Nothing would please me more," said Emma, although her face, solemn and gloomy belied her statement.

Nevertheless, the following day, she, Elizabeth, and Nell were at the coach stop, with their bags packed and ready to depart. The coach appeared around a corner. It was a large conveyance, with room for about a dozen travelers.

As the door opened, she looked inside and noted to her annoyance that they would not be able to sit together. The coachman leapt down from his perch and greeted them with a tip of his hat.

"Top of the mornin' ma'am," he said, with a pronounced Irish accent. "And which of youse lovely ladies will be travelin' with me today?"

"Why, all of us, of course," said Nell.

The coachman looked concerned. He turned and peered into the stationary coach. "I say- you! Mister with the mustachio there. You need to move over to allow these here ladies to join us in comfort."

"Of course," he said in a pronounced Italian accent, smiling genially. The gentleman with the moustache rose, tipped his hat, as he moved to a spot that would allow the three ladies to sit together. He sat beside Emma, and on the other side, Lizzie, beside - as though this had not been pre-planned - beside ... D'Arcy Hamilton.

Emma looked at the man with the Italian accent, and everything about him reminded her of Federico, her long lost lover. He had a twinkle in his eye, filled with some mischief, she imagined.

Nell climbed aboard first to prepare a spot for herself between the two ladies. Nell was not merely a deft hand at organizing the necessaries for travel; she had a sixth sense for knowing where Emma would like to sit. Lizzie stepped up next, aided by the driver.

She gathered her skirts and leapt up, exposing her ankle as she did, causing two of the elderly ladies in the carriage to gasp behind their gossiping fans.

Finally, Emma entered, far more dignified, and sat between this mustachioed stranger and Nell. D'Arcy Hamilton rose to greet them and began to negotiate a way to change seats so that he could sit beside Lizzie.

"I say! You are departing London as well, then? How fortuitous!" said D'Arcy. He appeared to be speaking to Emma but he was looking with saucer-eyes at Lizzie. Lizzie, of course, knew exactly what she was doing and immediately turned to him, squeezing his hand affectionately. Lizzie was absolutely without guile and her every emotion played on her face with the innocence of a newborn lamb.

A hubbub began to take over the interior of the carriage before their bags were deposited on top. However, after several minutes of confusion, everyone was seated where they ought to be. The stranger was careful not to offend and kept to himself for the first several post stops. He smiled when she looked at him, and Emma smiled when she noticed him looking at her.

Did he know about her awful tragic failed engagement? It was hard to know. Perhaps news travels all over the world if it is bad enough or embarrassing enough. Emma was feeling besieged by her own thoughts and never gave a thought to her duty as chaperone to Lizzie who was scandalously chatting openly with D'Arcy. Before she knew it, Nell was fast asleep beside her, lulled by the forward momentum of the carriage. The gentleman beside her seemed to be smiling unnecessarily, and before long she was curious about why he was so happy.

She looked at him and he looked shyly back. "I beg your pardon," he said, in a pronounced Italian accent. Emma was intrigued. As peculiar as it was to meet a gentleman on a carriage, she was amused that he appeared to be so similar to the cause of her sadness these many months. It was nearly a year since Federico had vanished from her life and she felt it was time to move on, and yet nothing in the capital had interested her even remotely.

"I see you are Italian," she ventured.

"Yes," he smiled. "I am from Verona. A small town in northern Italy. My name is Cavaliere Alberto Zobenigo. Veneziano nobile."

"I see," she said dryly. "And what on earth would possess any self-respecting Italian to come to these foggy isles?"

He chuckled. "I was going to ask leave of you to speak, but I see that you have already granted me that honor. I am on what we like to call 'il grande viaggiò.' It is sort of a rite of passage for a young nobleman from my country. You see, I love to travel, and have wanted to do this for many years. Consequently, several months ago, I begged my father to give me leave to travel abroad. I am travelling with only my valet, Carlo, who is sitting atop this carriage. As such, I am alone here."

"And how do you find the English? Congenial, I trust?"

"They are very kind. Of course, I have had some difficulty in gaining access to good society, but that is natural. I am in your debt to you for granting me this privilege."

Emma was taken aback. "What privilege?" she asked. Her thoughts were going very quickly and she was tending toward offense because of her past experience with Italian bounders. She wanted nothing to do with that experience, and yet this man, who seemed so like Federico, was quite kind. She decided to introduce herself.

"Forgive me, I forget myself. My name is Emma Shaftesbury, of Godington Manor in Kent. Perhaps you know our area?"

"I do not. I am just on my way to Dover to travel to France. I will be on my way to Paris within the week."

"Oh, you will love it. There is so much to see there." As she said this, Emma became aware that this man was more attractive than she had at first thought. Something inside her pushed her to learn more about him. She gazed at him. He had a beautifully styled moustache that did remind her of her lost love and hope of happiness. He also had the most beautiful blue eyes, surrounded by the longest, darkest, and most lush eyelashes. They batted almost to his cheeks as he smiled at her. He had a perfect olive complexion that set off his very long, deep amber-colored hair. His figure, while not overly tall, was very well turned out and, by the cut of his clothing, clearly manufactured in London's Savile Row, he was very well built. Something stirred inside her, and she noticed she had his full attention, his eyes, darting from one feature to another in her rather more than usually well-dressed self. Despite herself, she smiled at him.

"I say, Mr. Zobenigo, if you go to France, you must visit this most beautiful dress I have ever seen."

"That sounds wonderful. As you can see, I am most interested in clothing and the new cuts that are offered. I visited your Savile Row and asked one of the more interesting tailors to make this suit for me. I find it travels well and, given the mercurial nature of the weather in your country, it is an entirely appropriate attire for this cold climate. But I am very interested in what the French call 'haute couture'. Are you familiar with this?"

"Well, I know of it, but, of course, being English, I am likely to view their work as scandalous." She was saying this without really listening or even paying attention to what she was saying. Suddenly she caught herself and decided to say something scandalous.

"I saw a dress in a shop on the Champs Elysée called "Au Petit Dunkerque", which I once thought should be my wedding dress. I had a dream that the man who would marry me would find that dress and bring it to me. I cannot imagine getting married without it."

Alberto Zobenigo laughed at her scandalous talk. "I say, you are the most determined young lady I have ever met."

"Forgive me," said Emma.

"Dear me, no!" he countered. "It is most refreshing. And I promise you that I will find that dress and learn your lesson."

Sadly, at the moment, the coach pulled up in Canterbury's main coach stop. The sound of the creaking wheels was amplified in Emma's head and the opportunity to get to know this interesting and beautiful man was going to be lost.

"If you do see it, give it my regards," she said.

"If I see what? The dress?"

Emma nodded. Alberto laughed aloud. "It is gold...."

He rose, taking her hand in his, and she noticed how powerful and large his hands were. In his hands, hers looked rather like a doll's hand. He stood above her, and looked deep into her eyes. He took on a serious tone all of a sudden, and looked deeper into her eyes.

"I will see you again, Miss Shaftesbury. I make you this pledge." Emma was flustered by this sudden expression of something akin to affection from a man she hardly knew. She felt her face flush with emotion, and the smile that spread across his face was magnificent. "What is the name of that shop?"

"Au Petit Dunkerque," she said breathlessly. He smiled, clearly committing it to memory. Then, he backed away from her, turned with an almost military precision and left the coach, bound, it seemed, for Paris across the channel.

She watched his departing head, beautifully coiffed hair, and powerful broad shoulders and pondered how her good fortune could have suddenly turned so sad.

But, she also realized this was one of those lightning bolts of emotion she had, caused by her emotional nature following the embarrassing and humiliating loss of her fiancé a year before. She decided to let this Italian go and carry on home. She settled back in her seat, still warm with emotion, and closed her eyes so as not to see any more of him.

"I say, Emma," said her sister whom she thought had been asleep for this entire time. "That was a peculiar interaction. And as your chaperone, I must say I object." Emma turned her head suddenly toward her sister, and saw the broad smile across her face.

"You are a nasty vixen!" said Emma, embarrassed. As she turned away to sleep, she noted that Lizzie's hand was in D'Arcy Hamilton's strong grasp.

"He was more than usually handsome though, I must say. I observed his fine legs through my sleeping eyes. And he has much to recommend him. Still, he is a cad. He is an Italian and, you know what La Fontaine says about the cat."

"I'm sure I have no idea what you are talking about," said Emma.

"Once burnt, twice shy," she said, a smile breaking across her face.

Emma was not as amused as Elizabeth seemed to be by this comment. "It is immaterial, sister," said Emma in an annoyed tone. "I shall find myself a handsome English gentleman with acres and acres of land and funds forever. As mother did."

"Methinks the lady doth protest too much," said Elizabeth with a sly smile, looking at D'Arcy, who laughed. She had been reading rather too much of late, and her literary allusions were an annoyance to Emma who kept her romances in her boudoir, but rarely read anything else other than the Bible. She was perplexed at the worldliness of little Elizabeth, especially since she had rarely ventured much farther than her own lands. Nevertheless, she turned away and went to sleep.

Unbeknownst to Emma, Elizabeth had made plans with D'Arcy Hamilton and was planning on calling on him once they reached Kent.

Chapter 15. A Package in the Post

Both young sisters quickly grew tired of the country, and after a week, they both agreed to return to London. As Emma soon discovered, D'Arcy had returned, leaving Elizabeth with nothing to do.

In London, they enjoyed themselves greatly. Lizzie, who had long ago been planning to marry D'Arcy Hamilton, managed to find ways to encounter him at the homes of elderly aunts and solicitors. She was uncanny in her pursuit of this cad, despite the stories that were still circulating about his terrible reputation. She declared on more than one occasion that, even if he was a cad, she was the one to tame him. Emma endeavored to convince her otherwise - once a bounder, always a bounder, she said - and gave the sagest advice over dinners at the house on Belgrave Square that served as their London home.

"I seek only that you avoid scandal, Lizzie," said Emma over a delightful roast pheasant, one day, having endured her outings and visits to D'Arcy Hamilton for nearly a month. "Once a young lady's reputation is ruined, it cannot be un-ruined."

"Advice from the ruined," murmured Lizzie, apparently unaware that her sister could hear her.

Emma was furious at this rudeness and the clear disregard her younger sister was showing to her. Matilda, the elderly aunt with whom they were living, was as oblivious of any of the goings-on under her roof as any lady of good breeding could possibly be. Although she could not be sure, Emma believed Lizzie had been alone with D'Arcy Hamilton for several hours only a week before in their parlor, and she was not about to stand having her dearest friend and young sister ruined by this man she clearly viewed as nasty and petty.

Nevertheless, in her soberer moments, she had to admit she had never had any real conversation with him, relying on the slights and jibes of the petty London society members who seemed to revel in the destruction of one of their own. Nevertheless, as a woman scorned, (or so she had dubbed herself), she was doing her best to protect Lizzie from her basic urges, remembering this was what had ruined her own chances at wedding.

Indeed, at twenty-two, Emma Shaftesbury had resigned herself to a lifetime of spinsterhood. Nevertheless, having her nose rubbed in it by a saucy sister was not the sort of thing she could abide. Not yet. She had not yet sunk so low.

"You will stop that sort of talk at once!" said Emma rather more forcefully than she had intended. The look of shock of Lizzie's face let Emma know her words had struck a chord, and that she had cut her to the quick.

Indeed, Lizzie put her hand to her cheek as though she had been slapped. The look of shock and surprise on her face was almost as arresting to Emma as it had been for Lizzie, and Emma felt terrible when the tears began to flow down her cheeks.

"My heavens, Elizabeth. Whatever is wrong?" Emma had decided to try to adopt the style of inflection of the spinster aunt, Matilda, who was rarely seen in public and largely kept to her rooms on Belgrave Square.

Lizzie could not speak for several minutes. When she had calmed herself sufficiently, she looked at Emma and opened her mouth as if to speak. But the tears were flowing too much and she simply was unable.

"Lizzie!" said Emma, alarmed. "What is wrong?"

Emma took her sister's hand and held it tight while her sister wept. After several minutes, she looked into Emma's eyes. "He has proposed to me," she said slowly. "And I know I cannot accept."

"Why ever not?" asked Emma.

"It is you, my heart," said Lizzie. "You are older than me and I cannot accept him. He is frightened to ask father for my hand because he is aware of the fear of seeming a cad. We both want you to be happy. Oh please, Emma, can we leave and go back home? I cannot bear this place any longer."

Emma was taken aback. Her sister was feeling her pain almost as much as she felt it herself. Emma had no desire to quash her fondest desires, but she also did not want her to experience the horror of being jilted as she had.

"My heart, we can depart tomorrow at the first light if that is your wish!" she said.

Lizzie dried her tears and hugged her sister. "Thank you, my darling sister," she said. "I just do not know what to do with my predicament. He is eager to make me his, and yet I know full well that father would deny him. I know you are aware of his reputation, but Emma, I know him so well. It is not true, of course. Idle speculation and gossip from the unkindest elements. This is true."

Emma herself had heard about him ruining two young ladies before Lizzie had even become aware of his existence. D'Arcy was a cad and this reputation was well-deserved, for she had it on good authority that these tales were true. Nevertheless, she held her tongue.

"There is nothing to be done at this moment, but I warrant a little patience would do you well."

Lizzie laughed, knowing full well this was her worst trait. She was never able to wait for anything. She demanded satisfaction with every moment of her life. Still, the two ladies prepared to leave for Kent the next morning. Emma informed Aunt Tabitha, who, as she did with all news, reacted with shock and then resignation.

"I shall miss the callers and the sound of your young voices, but what can an older spinster do? I am resigned to my life of quiet dignity."

These words stabbed at Emma's heart, for she was well on her way to feeling the same way about her own life. She held her tongue though and decided to return.

It was less than two days later that their coach trundled into the circular drive in front of the manor. She had written by the last post the day before and knew that they were expected. Little did she know what awaited her though.

It was Sebastian who ran out to meet them. His dull face was aglow with anticipation. He carried with him a package.

"I say, Sebastian!" said Emma. "What is that in your hands?"

"It's for you, Emma!" he said. Emma took it from him as she watched the coachman and the servants take their luggage from atop the carriage. Nell was her usual well-organized self, overseeing the correct delivery of the baggage. Emma carried the parcel into the parlor and opened it gingerly. It had no distinguishing marks. It was a large package and was covered with brown paper, tied with an attractive bow, in the tricolor of France.

As her nervous fingers untied the ribbon, the paper fell away revealing a box with the distinguishing markings of "Au Petit Dunkerque," the shop where she had found the dress she hoped to be married in, and the source of her current misery. She had, in fact, concluded that she would never be married in that dress, and because of that, she would never be married at all. And yet, when she saw the label on the box, she felt weak.

"I cannot," was all she was able to muster.

Emma fell on to the divan and closed her eyes. Her mother, having been alerted to the fact that her two daughters had arrived home unexpectedly, rushed into the room just as Emma opened the box to reveal the beautiful golden gown she had loved so much in that little Paris shop.

"Oh mother! This is wonderful. You have no idea how much I have relished the idea of owning and wearing this beautiful gown. But how did you ever contrive to have it purchased?"

Anne was beside herself. She raised her hands to her mouth to cover her shock. And then, a second shock went through her body as she realized that Emma thought she had bought it. For a moment she contemplated taking responsibility for the dress, but dismissed it before she even spoke.

"Emma, I did not buy that dress for you," she said.

Emma looked at her mother in dismay. "What do you mean?"

"I mean that, as much as I adore it and adore you, I could never afford such a dear frock. It is simply not from me, or us, or any of the family."

Emma was dumbfounded. If her mother had not bought it, then who had? Was Federico coming back! Her heart missed several beats as the idea struck her. Dare she say it aloud?

"Who could have bought this then?" she wondered.

"Oh, it's Federico of course, you silly girl!" cried Lizzie as she pulled the gown out and put it against Emma's frame. "And it is absolutely perfect. I feel as though I had seen this before, from all the times you told me about it and darling, you did not do it justice!"

"Can I dare to hope?" said Emma quietly.

Lizzie heard her and laughed. "Of course you can. The only question that remains for me is if you can forgive him; if you can hear him out and see what his explanation for a year of silence could possibly be."

And indeed, it was true. Emma had grown accustomed to the idea that she would never marry, and certainly accustomed to the idea that she would never marry *Federico*. She had agonized for a year about him, and concluded his parents must have refused to allow him to marry her and he hadn't the gumption to stand up to them and demand his rights as a man must do. She was not at all sure she didn't hate him, and so the idea of marrying a man simply because he bought a dress was anathema to her. It was unthinkable. It was horrifying, but it was hope. Not for her, but for Lizzie who would be free to marry her love.

Emma buried her head in her hands and wept for joy and sorrow. She had so many conflicting emotions she almost could not bear to stay awake. She flew from the room to her bed chambers and she crawled into bed. There she wept the tears of the damned.

She was literally between a rock and a hard place. Her sister now could be freed from this purgatory in which she lived, but the only way she could do it would be to enter into an agreement with a man for whom she had not only wept, but for whom she bore a kind of hatred. He who had treated her with disdain and disrespect was not a person she could ever enter into the bonds of holy matrimony without losing her soul. This was a conundrum she was unable to solve on her own. She went to sleep to calm her nerves.

A week later, once she had regained her decorum, a letter arrived in the mail. It was delivered to Emma's room with her breakfast by Nell with a twinkle in her eye.

"What is with you this morning, Nelly?" said Emma as she noticed this mischievous smile.

"Just a letter for you ma'am. From a secret admirer, I warrant."

Emma laughed. "Would that were true," she said with a yawn. Placing the breakfast tray on her lap, Emma proceeded to cut open the letter with the letter opener Nell had passed her, almost fearful that should it be bad news, she would plunge it into her stomach.

Emma pulled out the scented, lavender colored letter. She unfolded it and knit her brows. "This is indecipherable!" she said, looking at the scrawl over the bottom of the letter. "Who on earth is this from? What does it say? She tossed it at Nell who looked panicked. "I'll give it a try," she said, her hands trembling. Nell was able to read, haltingly.

"Dear Emma," she read. "I trust you received my little token. It was the correct frock then, was it? I shall provide you with my address in Verona so you can respond if the spirit should move you. I was delighted to make your acquaintance and my pledge is true: we will meet again, if it be your will. Yours...." and here, Nell faltered. "I'm sorry Miss Emma, but I cannot read what he wrote. It is 'A' and some letters and 'Z' and some letters."

Emma was confused. "A, and Z," she said slowly. "I cannot imagine who this could be from."

"It's from the gentleman who bought you the dress. He even asked if it was the right one. I think, mistress, if I may, it is from that Eye-talian gentleman on the coach to Canterbury. Do you remember him? He was frightfully talkative. Scandalous, almost. Of course I had me hands full on that voyage, what with D'Arcy Hamilton taking liberties to my right and this Eye-talian taking 'em to my left!"

Emma paused. She tried to remember this incident but it was cloudy in her memory. Slowly though, his moustache returned and then his broad shoulders. Then she remembered the beautiful blue eyes with the thick lashes and the olive skin. This man was as attractive as Adonis, she thought. More importantly, he was not Federico, a man she had grown to despise.

"Nell, darling," said Emma suddenly. "Would you be so good as to get Lizzie for me?"

"Of course, Miss Emma," said Nell. She flew out the door and returned only minutes later with a breathless Lizzie on her heels.

"Elizabeth, do you remember a swarthy Italian gentleman on the coach to London?" she asked.

"He got off at Canterbury," she said. "I remember it well as it was a day burned into my soul."

Emma was taken aback. A day burned into her soul? Emma herself could hardly remember it. "What do you mean?" she asked.

"That was the day I knew I loved D'Arcy. We spoke about all of our dreams and aspirations and I knew that day he was the man I must marry."

"Oh Lizzie!" said Emma. "That is something we really need to settle. I know he is charming. That is the problem. He has been this way with so many other young ladies and I do not know if you are any different from them."

"But I do!" she said interrupting Emma in her monologue. "D'Arcy pledged his troth to me and I know his word is good. You can see it in his eyes. And this man, this 'swarthy Italian' as you call him, is a delight too. In fact, I believe it was he who bought you that frock. Does it fit you, by the way?" she asked.

To her shock and amusement, and embarrassment, Emma realized she had simply stored the dress in her dressing chamber and forgotten about it. She had not worn it and had no idea if it fit her.

"Nelly!" she called, bringing Nell back into the room. "Could you be a dear and get that golden frock from the dressing chamber? I should try it on to make sure it is useful."

Nell ran to the dressing chamber and returned moments later with the dress. It was hanging on a wooden hanger and looked beautiful. Nell helped Emma out of bed and quickly tied her hair up, tossing her nightgown on to the bed, and helping her put on this magnificent dress.

When the dress was properly donned, she turned and looked in the mirror. She gasped. Then she burst into tears.

Nell, alarmed, looked at her in horror. "Mistress Emma, what is wrong?"

"Is this the image of a spinster?" she said.

"No of course not."

"Then I am not a spinster!" said Emma with force. "I will be married, and on my terms!"

"You will indeed!" said Nell. "We can see to that."

"I just need to write back to this gentleman. But what is his name?"

"The Eye-talian? It was Alberto. I remember that because it was near to my brother Albert."

"Of course! Alberto Zobenigo. He is a nobleman from Verona. How true." Still dressed in the golden gown, Emma flew to her writing table and began her first letter to this mysterious Italian who had read the handwriting on her soul. She wrote, as she always did, with an open heart.

> "Dear Alberto (I pray you will allow me this liberty):" she wrote. "I received the dress and to my consternation, I could not figure out who had sent it to me. It was not mother, and due to many unfortunate things in my past, there

were a number of undesirable characters who could have been responsible for buying this lovely dress. And you were the last but most wonderful culprit. Thank you for your abundant generosity. I hope to remain at the very least, pen pals. I remain, yours truly, Emma Shaftesbury, Godington Manor, Kent, England."

In a flash, she had sealed the letter with her stamp and begged Nell to post it with all speed.

For the remainder of the day, she wore the dress, and received compliments on the gown from all who saw her. Although she stayed at home, she had visitors from many of the ladies in that area, and all were amazed at the beauty of the dress.

When evening came, Emma found her mood had turned, perhaps permanently, from gloomy to overwhelmingly joyous. She was hopeful for the future and happy things were so clear ahead of her. She knew, somewhere deep within her soul that this man was probably incredibly wealthy and the purchase of this gown was probably only an afterthought to him. But the gesture meant the world to her and she was immensely grateful for the kindness shown to her. Her sleep resumed and she began to feel the world was not the deep pit of despair in which she had lived for the past year. There was hope: even if it was just in seeing Lizzie married.

Chapter 16. A Stranger in Our Midst

Elizabeth Shaftesbury, the second daughter, had never been a model child. She was clever and willful, independent and thoroughly worrisome to her father, and a decided joy to her mother. Elizabeth, and not Emma, she had concluded, was the one who would live the life of excitement. Consequently, as is the habit of parents, they were less than rigid in their upbringing of their second daughter.

It was also fortuitous for her, if not for the family's fortunes, that the son and heir, young Sebastian, was dull-witted and slow, his speech unclear, and his slovenliness notable to all who met him. He preferred the company of the local lads, children of the farmers and craftsmen of the area, to those of his peers. He showed none of the abilities of his two sisters, of his father or his mother. As a result, both of the parents depended for some of the things normally asked of a son from their daughters.

Knowing this was one of the things she could do, Elizabeth awoke on a Saturday morning and dressed without the help of her maid, Ruth, who was a lazy girl in any case, and took it as her right to be able to sleep in on a Saturday morning. This disturbed Nell, who was responsible and in a similar position, but was fastidious and took it as an insult when her co-worker neglected her duties. Nevertheless, this was the state of affairs at Godington Manor, with Ruth lying in her bed at nine o'clock and Lizzie sneaking out the servant's entrance, fitting the trap and driving it herself to meet D'Arcy Hamilton at the *Baying Hounds Inn.*

By now it was after noon and luncheon was being served in the dining room when it was first discovered that Lizzie had disappeared. All was in turmoil and Ruth was being questioned. Of course, she knew nothing, as nothing can be learned about Lizzie's whereabouts from the safety of one's bed. And all would have remained in this state of turmoil, and Ruth would have lost her station, had not a bizarre and fortuitous event taken place.

What happened was so untoward, so unpredictable, so bizarre, that the annals of English country gentlemen had never recorded such an event. And doubly so was it said in subsequent years, that certainly two such events had never happened to the same gentleman. That was certain. But at Godington Manor, it had happened once and it would happen again.

Invasion! By the Italians! This time, it was a stranger. No family friend from the Grand Tour. This was a gentleman who had never once set foot in the manor house, and met neither the lord nor the lady of the manor.

And yet, in the midst of the tumult caused by the disappearance of the younger daughter and the consequent confusion, there appeared a man on horseback in the main courtyard out in front of the manor. This man was dressed in a top hat and was draped in a black cape against the weather, although it was June and quite pleasant. He had a pronounced and rather elaborate moustache.

His stallion was a pure-bred Arabian, glistening with sweat from a long and furious ride. The gentleman himself looked half crazed and exhausted from his journey. Nobody within the manor was expecting him, and yet he was certain this was his destination. He had ridden hard for nearly two days without a break and was bound and determined to arrive before something bad happened.

He was the young and handsome nobleman from Verona, in northern Italy, and he had the tell-tale long blonde hair of his northern race, with the olive complexion of his southern forebears. He was well-made and strong, his chest broad and his shoulders wide. He was not overly tall, but powerful in many other ways. His hair was worn long as was the fashion in Italy at the time, and his top hat was worn with a slight tilt, in the European fashion. His clothing beneath the cape was a well-made English suit from Savile Row.

When he arrived in the courtyard, he leapt from his horse as though he were a vaulter, with such gymnastic ability that it would strike fear into any foe who should meet him on the battlefield. And yet, this was no battlefield. He was on a domestic quest.

"View Halloo!" he shouted, having read somewhere that this would bring servants in an English manor. To his consternation, nothing happened. However, he did not know about the tumult that was taking place within, due to the disappearance of Elizabeth Shaftesbury. He strode with purpose to the door, his boots making a pleasant sound against the cobblestones. He raised the massive knocker, in the shape of a lion's head, and let it fall. He heard the echo through the house and only then did he begin to hear of the mayhem within.

Simons, the butler, appeared at the door, unruffled despite the war waging behind him.

"Good day, my good man," began the stranger. "I am seeking the lord and lady of the manor. I am Signore Alberto Zobenigo, Veneziano, and I wish to speak to the lord and the lady about their daughter --"

"But she's gone amiss!" said Simons, cutting him off. He saw several servants dashing up and down the large marble staircase.

"I beg your pardon. Who has gone amiss?" he said, confused. The fact of the matter was Alberto Zobenigo had not ridden without halt from Verona, but he did ride from the *Baying Hounds Inn* where he met an acquaintance of his, D'Arcy Hamilton, who was in conversation with a young woman named Elizabeth Shaftesbury, in a proper sitting room, and in absolutely no mortal danger.

"Elizabeth Shaftesbury!" shouted Simons nearly in his ear.

"Well then, I bring thee tidings of great joy which shall be unto all generations," said Alberto magnanimously. He had learned this phrase from reading the *King James Bible* and was relishing the chance to use it.

"Come again?" said Simons, wondering what kind of popish devil stood here in front of him, clad in a foppish top hat and a devilish black cape, lined with blood red satin, and spouting the Word of God.

"I say I bring thee-"

"Yes, you mentioned that. What is your confounded news?"

"Miss Shaftesbury is at the *Baying Hounds Inn*, in no mortal danger whatsoever, and so I bid thee comfort ye, my people." Once again, he was paraphrasing the *King James Bible*.

Simons stepped back and slammed the door on the Italian's face. Moments later, the door opened and Sir Rufus Shaftesbury appeared at the door.

"What the devil do you want?" he said, furious.

The young Italian gentleman stepped back and held his hand out in a gesture of surrender. "I want to speak to the Lord of the Manor, Sir Rufus Shaftesbury."

"Your wish is granted!" said Sir Rufus.

"Ah! So that is who you are?"

"Righto," said Sir Rufus.

"I have seen your daughter and she is in no peril whatever. So, fear not, for she is blessed among women. She is under the care of one D'Arcy Hamilton, a man of the purest and best morals. He and she are hoping to marry. But I am here to speak to you about another matter altogether: the matter of your eldest daughter, Emma."

"Look, mate, we are in a bit of a bind just at the moment. Do you think you could bring your prepared speech at a more opportune time?"

"No I could not. I have ridden for nearly a week, and I will be heard!" he said forcefully.

This was Sir Rufus's turn to step back at the force of this young man's will.

At that moment, Emma herself appeared in the doorway. She recognized

Alberto at once by his silhouette, and took note that he was far more beautiful than she had remembered. His perfect teeth glistened white and his red lips accentuated the olive of his skin. If there were such a thing as love at second sight, she would have fallen instantly this time around. She felt weak.

"I am Alberto Zobenigo, and I would like to make the acquaintance of your daughter Emma. I admire her very much. I had the good fortune to meet her on a coach several months ago. I will not leave your door until I know I have not come in vain."

In the madness that was going on, Emma too lost herself. "You have not come in vain!" she cried. "For I am here, Alberto Zobenigo. I do not really know how to pronounce your name but I admire you for your kindness, and your care and your terrible penmanship and your beautiful hair and your well-formed figure, and your generosity and you understanding. I will be delighted to be your friend as long as my parents agree."

Alberto was astounded at the force of her vigor and her ardor. He was overwhelmed and filled with joy to such an extent that he could barely contain himself.

"But I don't even know who you are," said a totally befuddled Sir Rufus.

"I will go and fetch your younger daughter Elizabeth now for you," he said, and he leapt to his horse and charged off like a Knight of the Round Table. Within the hour, he had returned with an angry and complaining Elizabeth, seated uncomfortably behind him on his Arabian steed. She was livid and scornful of his actions, taken without her permission as he abducted her and returned her to her home.

"I thought you were a gentleman!" she called to him as the door slammed in his face.

Alberto returned to the inn and looked at D'Arcy. "Is the elder daughter as mad as the younger?" he asked, flinging himself on a divan.

"Quite!" said D'Arcy. "That is what is so frightfully loveable about them."

"Ai, Mamma Mia!" he said, in Italian. "Questi inglesi sono pazzi![10]"

"È vero, amico,[11]" said D'Arcy in flawless Italian.

---

[10] Oh My Mother. These English are mad!
[11] It's true my friend.

Chapter 17. A Stroll in the Garden

For days after the first meeting with Sir Rufus, Alberto Zobenigo stayed at the *Baying Hounds Inn*, only a few miles from Godington Manor. He had shown his best side to his would-be father-in-law, and felt that progress would shortly happen. However, he was disappointed when he received no word from the family, including Emma, for days. Little did he know that bedlam had once again erupted at Godington Manor when he had retrieved Elizabeth, or that he had put himself at the center of a family squabble that would take days to work out.

On the third day, however, Emma Shaftesbury finally remembered the reasons why all this had come to pass. The strange Italian man, the most perfectly formed Italian since Michelangelo finished carving *David*, which she had seen but barely glanced at when in Florence, was this man named Alberto Zobenigo. And she was overcome with a desire to know him better. He had shown up at her door, asking to be formally introduced to her, and the only time she had ever spoken to him, in a coach headed for Canterbury, which had been very pleasant, had been less than world-shaking. Certainly not life altering. Their conversation had been pedestrian and dull; she had told him about the dress she had fallen in love with, and he, unlike any other person, had listened. Where he differed from others was that he had gone there and possibly mortgaged his soul to get it for her, mail it to her anonymously. This left her with the horror that it could have been sent by Federico. He had, unwittingly, filled her with dread, which was assuaged when he turned up and claimed her as his own.

    The issue, to her, was not whether the buyer of the dress was Federico, because, although it would have been a sorrowful addendum to the story of the beautiful dress, she would never have married him regardless. The more important issue was that this new suitor who reminded her so much of the love she had given to Federico, had claimed he loved her at first sight. The irony for her was that when she saw him in the full light of day, clad in a cape and a top hat, she felt the feelings in her stir, making her wonder if love at first sight was a thing that existed. Second sight, that is. To that end, she resolved to figure out who he was and to offer an olive branch to him.

Emma dashed off a note and sent it to the *Baying Hounds Inn*, inviting him to see their gardens.

> Dear Alberto: I would like to take some time to understand the man who would bring me a Paris gown, and abduct my sister. You are a man of many mysteries and I should like to unravel your narrative thread. To that end, I should like to invite you to see our gardens, which are quite lovely. Would you be free to join me tomorrow or the next day for tea? Yours truly, Emma Shaftesbury

Godington Manor had wonderful gardens, and, even for England, where gardens were a point of as much pride as the building itself, it was outstanding. Furthermore, she knew Italians could appreciate this wonder of nature. A number of Italians she had encountered on her travels had mentioned how much they appreciated English country gardens. Although her offer was clearly a clumsy means of meeting and talking, she felt no remorse for her decision. In fact, she was rewarded when an answer was dispatched by the first return post.

> My dear Emma: I should be delighted to join you. I am a great admirer of English country gardens and would relish a guided tour through one of the finest. I would be remiss if I did not mention, as well, my eagerness to know my guide. So, by your leave, I shall appear tomorrow around two. Is that

acceptable? Yours, Alberto Zobenigo, Veneziano nobile

The following day, she, with the help of Elizabeth, her mother, and Nell, sat dressed in a modest yet fetching frock of lilac, with puffed sleeves and simple conical skirts. She wanted to look modest in view of the liberties she had known other Italian men to take. When breakfast was cleared away, Emma went to the fortepiano and began to play her finest Mozart sonatas. She knew some of the simpler works and on a slightly overcast day like today, she thought, Mozart, with his light and joyful little melodies, was the perfect accompaniment.

She became lost in the music. Such is the nature of Mozart, and she did not notice when the door rang and Alberto Zobenigo presented himself at the door of Godington Manor in dashing English fox-hunting attire. She failed to notice the conversations that took place at the door, the butler Simons who ushered young Alberto into the parlor where she was playing with great vigor. He simply stood and waited for her to finish. It took nearly ten minutes before she noticed he was standing there.

Emma finished her sonata with great flair, using the sustain pedal to make the last few notes ring. Her knee was pushing hard on the pedal when she finally looked around and saw Alberto smiling at her, his face a mask of joy. He began to applaud and Emma was suddenly horrified at this invasion of privacy.

"That was very beautiful," said Alberto. Emma was struck dumb and simply sat there, lowering her knee from the pedal to silence the ringing last chord.

"I am very sorry you had to listen to this nonsense," she said solemnly at great length.

"Not at all, Emma," he said. "Have you ever played a pianoforte?"

"I have never had the pleasure," said Emma, rising from the instrument.

"It has so much more delicacy," he said. "I think this music, this Mozart music, was intended for the pianoforte."

Emma, sensing he was implying she had played in too masculine a fashion, was slightly put off by his comment but let it go. She was very happy to see him, regardless of his habit of sneaking into a room unannounced.

"Should we go to the garden?" she suggested.

"I would be delighted," he said, and he really looked as though he really would be delighted. It was a curious thing about this man. He was not a grand romantic in the way Federico had been, but he was solid and sensible, and honest, by all accounts. He looked at Emma and when he looked, he looked as though he were in love with her. He had done things that were so romantic, but done them in a modest and quiet way which was the antithesis of Federico. In virtually every way, the signs pointed to her falling in love with this beautiful male.

She took him by the hand and led him to the garden. "It is really the height of the season this month," she said, knowingly.

"If you look along this vista, you can see the nearest manor house," said Emma. "It is in reality nearly two miles off but there is some optical illusion that makes it feel as though it were only a few hundred yards away."

"It is a very nice home, I think," he said admiring the view. "Who is its owner?"

"Oh, it is unowned at the moment. Or rather, unoccupied. It had been the home of the dowager Duchess of Kent until her death at a great age last year." Emma did not dare to mention her high hopes of purchasing it the year before, and could not mention her hopes of purchasing it because of these memories, of the dreams she had of living there with Federico. Nevertheless, she was thinking it when Alberto approached her, and, from desperately close behind her, whispered, "Emma, I want you to know that from the moment I laid eyes upon you, I have not had you out of my mind. I went to Paris full of hope and when I sent you that dress, I very nearly did not write because I was struck by what a fool I was. I know the rules of British decorum and I knew I had transgressed. However, I am still so happy you have accepted me for my flaws."

"Of course," she said. She wanted to say more but her mind was racing, hearing these blandishments. She simply smiled.

"I hope I have not overstepped my rights at any point in this, even though I know I have done some mad things."

"No, Alberto, you haven't yet," said Emma, pointing out the clematis growing up the side of the wall in front of them. "I feel that we are getting along very well, and to be honest, I never dreamed I would find a man as good and true as you, and that is the honest feeling I have about this issue. So, please, worry not about it. Let us enjoy this day."

Alberto was overjoyed and grasped Emma by the waist and pulled her to him. He kissed her on the hand with all the ardor of a man driven mad by lust. Emma was shocked, not because she did not enjoy it but because it was a very sudden and passionate gesture and, as an Englishwoman, she was unused these displays of overt affection.

She pulled away, and Alberto realized his mistake. The culture clash suddenly was clear to him and he too pulled away. "I am deeply sorry, Emma," he said.

"No, I understand," she said, wiping her hand. "I am just unused to such displays. You see, in English society, one does not show affection is such physical ways. And, I suppose, I was a trifle unnerved by your display. I must ask you to remember yourself when you are in my presence." Emma rose and headed back to the manor.

Alberto, chastened, followed behind her, feeling every bit the fool he felt he was. "Perhaps I should return to the inn," he said, embarrassed.

"Yes, that would be best," she replied, although she longed to embrace him. She turned, took his hand in hers and shook it vigorously. "I shall be in touch with you presently. Thank you for visiting Mr. Zobenigo."

Chapter 18. Return to the Baying Hounds

Several days later, after Emma had recovered herself, she was sitting in the music room, idly playing on the fortepiano, when Elizabeth entered. "Emma, I need your help. Would you like to go to see your Italian gentleman? I believe he is staying at the *Baying Hounds Inn*."

Emma was taken aback at this show of selflessness from her normally selfish sister. "I should like that very much; I miss him, as you know."

"I can imagine. I saw the embrace you shared out in the garden. I dare say it was quite passionate."

Emma blushed, trying to maintain her demeanor. "It was an attack on my person, and not an embrace, for I was in no way responsible for that untoward advance. Nonetheless I must say, I know he intended only good to come from it. Nevertheless, I am not to be held responsible."

"Methinks the lady doth protest too much," said Elizabeth, laughing. "Come with me, Emma. Let's visit our beaux."

"Our beaux? What do you mean?"

"Oh, D'Arcy is there too."

"I see." The lady was not quite so selfless as she had appeared a minute before. Emma smiled. "I'll go make sure the trap is ready," she said.

When they arrived in the courtyard of the country inn known as the *Baying Hounds Inn*, Elizabeth asked Simmons to hold the trap for an hour or two while they paid their respects. Emma climbed down unaided and entered the inn. She inquired if they had an Italian gentleman staying with them.

"Indeed we do, if you must know. Are you with the constabulary?" said the innkeeper, laughing jovially.

"Oh my, no!" said Emma, with some shock. "I was merely going to pay a social call for him. Why would you think I were here to arrest him?"

"I reckon I don't know. I suppose it's just that them Europeans is in the habit of gettin' theyselves in trooble. Leastways when they is palling around with Sir D'Arcy." He laughed heartily at his jape, making Emma uncomfortable. "And so, who should I say is callin'?"

"My name is Emma Shaftesbury, of Godington Manor."

"Oy! To the manor born are ye?" he continued with his coarse witticisms.

"Why yes," said Emma, without any sense that she was egging on his feeble attempts at humor. "But please announce us if you please."

"Us? Who's us?" he asked, genuinely confused. Emma looked around and noticed that Elizabeth had not followed her in the inn. "I say, my sister was here a minute ago."

"Oh yes, Miss Elizabeth is your sister, then is she? We're quite familiar with her in this inn." Again, his tasteless joke fell on deaf, but rather concerned ears. "She'd be up there with Sir D'Arcy."

Emma was quite sure that D'Arcy Hamilton was no peer of the realm, but it seemed he had convinced the innkeeper of his lofty rank, likely on the pretext of not needing to pay. She put that out of her mind and stood her ground.

"Please announce me," she said, proceeding to the drawing room of the inn, away from the stench of ale coming from the tavern.

She sat herself in a stuffed chair by the window, with her back to the door. In no more than a few minutes, Alberto came bounding down the stairs.

Breathlessly, he approached her. "Miss Shaftesbury," he almost whispered.

Emma turned, smiling. Her eyebrow was arched in a stern manner but there was a smile both on her lips and in her eyes. She was clearly delighted to see Alberto, and the look on his face belied his eagerness to see her too.

"I must tell you, I have been living in Inferno for the past three days, atoning for my misdeed in your beautiful English garden. I am terribly sorry for that display. I am only now learning the rules of etiquette in English society. Sir D'Arcy has been instructing me in the finer points. And he is a wonderful teacher, and has a diligent student in me."

"Alberto, D'Arcy Hamilton is no gentleman. In fact, I believe he is a cad of the worst type. A bounder. And I would not take his advice if I were you. You may learn the absolute worst rules in the world from him. But I trust that you, as a noble Venetian, would know how to treat a lady. I have only had the greatest respect from you, notwithstanding your ardor in the garden." Emma had to laugh at the misery she had plunged this poor wonderful man for days simply for stealing a kiss. She took his hand in hers and he nearly fainted from the contact. "It is with only the greatest of respect that I take your hand, my friend," she said, looking deep into his eyes. She saw the look of passionate love in his eyes and suddenly, without control or without any nod to decorum, she found herself moving to kiss him on the lips.

Alberto was not only prepared, but returned her passion with a fiery passion of his own. "Oh Emma!" he said. "Tell me you will marry me!"

"I will, I will!" she said with passion. "I love you very much indeed." And with that, she kissed him on his full red lips. It was a feeling she had only dreamed about and she was happier at this moment than she could have ever dreamed she would be. "Of course I love you. Of course I shall marry you."

"Oh Emma, I am so happy!" he cried, kissing her again full on the lips and grasping her tightly around the waist. "You are the fulfillment of my dreams! I will never love another!"

Suddenly, the passion gave way to embarrassment as D'Arcy Hamilton appeared in the doorway followed shortly by Elizabeth. It appeared they may have been looking for a similar private spot, and stumbled upon the passionate Italian and his newly minted fiancée. They instantly pulled apart, horrified to be caught *in flagrante*!

D'Arcy, on the other hand, used to being caught rather than catching others, smiled a huge grin. It looked rather as though his face would crack in two, he was so overjoyed at the discovery of their indiscretion. "Well, I think this room is filled to capacity," he said superciliously.

"Oh D'Arcy, stop it," snapped Elizabeth, who had not in fact seen what had been happening. "You stumble upon two innocents and all of a sudden there is the rape of the Sabines at work. You know very well we were looking for privacy in any case. So, wipe that look off your face."

The look on his face did in fact disappear, replaced with a look of fury and embarrassment on his face, making Emma afraid he would hit Elizabeth for her rudeness. But his temper was quashed as quickly as it had come up, and he looked to the two lovers and begged their forgiveness.

"I am sorry for my foolishness," he said. "It was most indiscreet and it shan't happen again." The two of them left abruptly, followed hot on their heels by Emma, horrified at her lack of sense.

In the trap on the way back to the manor, Emma was silent, brooding. "What is the matter with you, my dear? Did the Italian abuse you?"

"Oh heavens, no. But Lizzie, can you keep a secret?"

"Oh my dear. I have kept secrets from everyone for years. I am keeping one right this very minute!"

Despite her wit, Emma looked to Lizzie for help. "Lizzie, I kissed him. I kissed *him*. On the lips! I am simply mortified."

"Is that what D'Arcy was crowing about? Oh don't be silly. I've kissed D'Arcy on the lips dozens of times!"

Emma paused in her worry and looked at Lizzie. "Oh Lizzie, that is not good."

Lizzie laughed. "You worry so much, my dear Emma. Just remember love is an elusive thing, and the principal task of the young lady in good society is to entice a man to marry."

"But this is not the way to entice a man. Giving away precious things for free is a dangerous road to embark on, Lizzie. I trust you have not allowed him any further liberties!"

"Of course not, although I admit I have desires, probably more than you have."

"I want to hear nothing more on the subject, and I warrant you are not the right person to talk about this with, since your libertine values are incongruous with mine. But I wonder if I shouldn't go back and tell Alberto I have made a terrible mistake."

"Did you? Did you not get him to promise to marry you?"

"Why yes."

"And is that not your principal job? To entice a man of good standing in society to marry you?"

"I suppose so."

"He is of good standing is he not?"

"Yes."

"Then you must not think about it again. I suggest you talk to mother about it. You'd be surprised how wise she is in matters of the heart."

When Emma reached home, she flew to her writing desk and dashed off a quick note to Alberto.

> My dear Alberto:
> Much as I would desire nothing more than to be free with you in all matters, it is not the proper or correct way to proceed. I am writing to tell you that what we did – what I did – was wrong and I must atone for this. Asa result, I pledge to stay away from you until such time has passed that our mutual embarrassment has ebbed. You must understand that this kind of behavior and most especially the fact that we were caught red-handed by a cad, is a

particular humiliation. I shall be in touch at the end of my penance. Sincerely, Emma

Looking at her letter, she sealed it and ordered it delivered to the *Baying Hounds Inn*.

After she had regained her self-control, Emma sought out her mother for advice. She rarely did this and so Anne, her mother, was delighted to offer her pearls of wisdom on the subject.

Seated in her sewing room, Anne spoke solemnly to her daughter.

"Emma, I will tell you an experience I once had and let you decide what is right about this matter. But first let me ask you a few questions."

"Very well," said Emma.

"Are you in love with this Alberto fellow?" she asked.

"I believe I am, yes." She paused. "It is just that he is so unconventional that I cannot anticipate his actions. With an Englishman, we both know the rules of the game, but with Alberto, things seem so unpredictable."

"Perhaps it is because that is not a game, Emma. It is a mutual understanding. Games only confuse the issue."

"Well, of course. But you know what I intend. The truth is that I believe I am in love with Alberto."

"In that case, listen to this story and you tell me your thoughts on the subject," said Anne. "When I was a young girl, before I met your father, I was attending finishing school in Geneva. At one of the social events there, I met a young Frenchman who was visiting one of his elderly aunts in the country. We struck up a friendship - he helped me a great deal with my French - all of which I have since forgotten - and slowly, over the summer, we became close. Almost like best friends.

"We would attend social events together, always chaperoned, of course, and for one ball that was held at the estate of an ex-patriot Frenchman, Jean-Pierre - for that was his name - wore a scandalous Napoleonic jacket. This was at a time when Napoleon was seen as a terrible aggressor in Europe, and I was horrified. He explained that he was not doing anything that he felt was political - it was just the fashion that year in Paris and he had no feelings one way or the other about Napoleon. It was just the "mode", as he called it. I decided to take offense and, in a fury, I left the ball, and went home, never to admit him again.

"He wrote me several letters, but I returned them unopened. I still have no idea what he had said in his defense, but I ask you, Emma, did I do the right thing? I did what was determined to be correct according to our tradition, but he was not from my tradition, and so I have always wondered what would have happened if I had simply been open to ideas that were outside the normal circle of my narrow English schoolgirl values. What do you think? Bear in mind that I am very happy with your father, and that things worked out jolly well for me."

"I think that is a good lesson for me, but I am unsure about what was the right thing to do for you. If I stay true to my values, I may well marry happily."

"Is that the be-all, end-all of life?" said Anne. "What about passion, true love, and those feminine values. Do you think I could have experienced passion? I did my duty, sure enough, but I have always wondered whether I was true to my soul."

Emma was surprised to hear this from her mother, but simultaneously confused because of her perceived duties to her social class. "I confess, mother, you have confused me." She giggled a little but her mother did not smile. Emma rose and excused herself.

"Passion is a flower that is extremely delicate. You must handle it with the greatest care. I know because I am one who killed that flower by handling it carelessly."

She went to her writing desk and took out her quill. Spreading a piece of paper on the desk, she began to write:

"Dear Alberto: I have been a terrible fool and a foolish, prideful prude. I promised and then unpromised my hand to you. I now realize that I love you, but that our love is one of those uncommon things that falls out of the bonds of normal convention. Please come and ask for my hand, as I am desperately in love with you and cannot live without you.
    Yours truly, Emma Shaftesbury, Godington Manor."

Later, the following day, the post arrived and her second letter was returned unopened. On the front of the envelope was scrawled "don't stay here no more" in a rustic hand. Suddenly Emma knew she had done something terrible, something her mother had tried to warn her about. He had left.

A Foreign Affair

Once again, an Italian had humiliated her. She was in the depths of despair.

Chapter 19. Days of Turmoil

The news that Alberto Zobenigo had left the *Baying Hounds Inn* was devastating to Emma, mainly because it was totally unprepared and she was unaware that anything was wrong other than the letter she had unadvisedly sent upon her arrival at Godington Manor. She agonized about this decision for days, reading and re-reading the letter she had sent, and wondering what would have happened had he stayed just a bit longer.

Her misery was unabated several days later when there appeared in their courtyard a large cart with rubber tires. No one in the house had the slightest idea what was happening or what was under the many wrappings of this cart.

The cart driver was a Londoner, who seemed exhausted upon his arrival. He came to the servants' entrance begging for water and some help in moving his load.

A Foreign Affair

Simons, wanting to maintain the decorum that was habitual in the manor, demanded to know this man's business.

"Let me have my drink a while," said the driver. "I am mightily exhausted, and need just a few minutes to regain myself."

"Very well," said Simons. "But I need to know your business. My master has made no purchase that would justify this intrusion on our dignity."

Having finished his mug of water, the driver rose and looked around. "Did I say there was a purchase from this house?" he demanded. "I never said ought. And for your information I bear a gift for the lady of the house, one Miss Emma Shaftesbury. She does reside here, does she not?"

"As it happens she does, as if that were any of your affair," said Simons.

"Well, can you spare a couple of strong lads to help me with this 'ere pianoforte? I was unable to entice any of me own lads to make this journey."

Simons was surprised but decided to be cooperative. "Give me a few minutes to get some help and I need a moment to consult with Miss Shaftesbury and the master of the house." He bowed and left the room, utterly confused.

Moments later, he returned. "Nobody here made no purchase like what you described," he said with a note of finality. "So, in view of this news, I must ask you to remove yourself and your burden."

The driver was perplexed at the idea of returning with this heavy load. His cart looked not strong enough to make the journey back to London with a pianoforte onboard. "Sir, I beseech you," he said.

"I'm frightfully sorry, but there must be some sort of mistake."

"It's no mistake, mate. It is a gift from some Eye-talian gentleman. It's a Broadwood Piano made in London especially for Miss Emma Shaftesbury, a gift from ... one minute..." He rummaged in his satchel for the paper. "His name is Albert Zobenigo."

The poor man stumbled over the name, just as Emma entered the servants' quarter.

"What is all this excitement about?" she asked. "Did you say there was pianoforte delivered?"

"Why, mistress, but it is a mistake. A mistaken gift."

"From Alberto?" her eyes lit up.

"Yes mum," said the driver, wiping his mouth.

"Well, bring it into the parlor at once!" she ordered. Simons looked very confused. Then, switching his attitude, he said sternly. "You heard the lady. Bring it in at once!"

"Beggin' your pardon, sir, but it must weigh eighty stone. I canna lift it meself."

"Oh, very well," said Simons. "You, Rodney and Pete. You can help with this load if you please," he said, looking at the two lads sitting at the table, who normally worked as footmen. They looked none too pleased with the honor but rose and followed the carter to his wagon.

An hour later, the pianoforte was ensconced in the parlor, and Emma was joyously playing on it. As she pushed the keys for some of the higher notes, a sour tone was sounded. Emma rose, and looked inside. There was a letter wedged between some of the strings. She retrieved it and broke the seal quickly and deftly. It was a letter from Alberto.

"My darling Emma," it said. "I received your letter and I want to beg your pardon. I have received serious and frightful news from my family, that my mother is on the point of death with a serious illness, and so I must hasten with all speed to her side. I do hope you enjoy this pianoforte, though. It is London's finest, and I believe the Mozart music you had played earlier will sound beautiful on it. I will write to you from Italy. Your loving fiancé, Alberto Zobenigo, Veneziano."

Emma was overjoyed with the piano and the loving letter from Alberto, but at the same time, devastated that her lover, as she considered him, would leave for Italy again. On the other hand, Alberto referred to himself as her fiancé, which was a blessing.

To test his theory, she sat at the piano and began to play the Mozart sonata. It was, indeed entirely different on a pianoforte; far smoother and more melodious. She had heard tell that the composer Mozart was touring in London around that time, and although she knew this fellow was a hoax, it was said that he played beautifully. Rumor had it that this Mozart was actually the son of the great and deceased composer. Emma spent much of the next day playing this piece and others, learning the new mechanism of the sustain pedal which she played with her foot, and the other two pedals which, at first, she could not understand, but soon realized were the sostenuto (or soft) pedal. The middle pedal was a peculiar mechanism that held down only the notes she played with her fingers as she pushed the pedal, allowing certain tones to ring out.

By the third day, she had mastered the instrument and decided that she much preferred this subtle instrument, massive though it was, and virtually immovable. It had a cast iron frame, which allowed for a great tension on the strings, and great subtlety at the same time.

She was still playing when Nell entered with a letter. "From your beau!" she said excitedly.

Emma tore it from her hands, and ripped it open.

> "Dear Emma," it began. "I have received good news and excellent news. My mother, though once on the point of death, has recovered and is once more in charge of the household."

"What do I care?" said Emma to herself. "Tell me something about me!"

"The excellent news is that, having heard your many accomplishments, my family has wholeheartedly agreed that you should be my bride! I am absolutely overjoyed. My only query is that I know not whether to have an Italian wedding or an English one. Or, perhaps both! Do please respond as soon as you can, with your response and your preference as I am your servant and will do your bidding. I am forever yours,

     Alberto Zobenigo, Veneziano."

"Oh my heavens!" said Emma just as Elizabeth came in.

"May I try your new toy?" Lizzie asked, but then noticed the look on Emma's face. It was a look of heavenly joy. "What news on the Rialto?" she asked, quoting her favorite Shakespeare play, *The Merchant of Venice.*

"I have received news from abroad," said Emma. "Alberto has gained permission from his family to wed. To *wed* me! And he wants to know if we should have an Italian wedding or an English one... or both!" She burst into tears of joy saying this aloud. "Oh Lizzie! I am so happy. It seems my foolishness was not enough to dissuade him from marrying me."

"Yes I see. But darling. You really must write back and tell him that if he is in fact serious about this marriage, he must come back and formally ask for your hand. Father would not allow you to steal away with this unknown fellow without a formal request."

"You are right," said Emma, knowingly. "Now please help me to compose this epistle."

The two of them sat right down and composed the letter. Within minutes, it was signed, sealed, and sent on its way. It was essentially a demand for protocol. All the rules had to be heeded, and if he wanted to marry her, he must needs come to Godington Manor to state his intentions.

Nell entered the parlor with another letter. "A letter arrived for Miss Elizabeth Shaftesbury as well," she said. "It appears to be a letter from Alice Beddington, in London," she announced.

"Oh Nell! Shame on you for spying. Alice Beddington is the biggest gossip in all of London. She will surely fill me in on the juiciest news from society! Give it here!"

Lizzie tore open the letter and read avidly. Her eyes danced at the scandals that were erupting all over the capital. But then suddenly she clouded over. "No!" she cried, dropping the letter.

Alarmed, Emma ran to her sister. "What is the matter?" she asked anxiously.

"D'Arcy Hamilton is engaged."

"Well, of course. He is engaged to you."

"No! He is engaged to that baggage, Kitty Clendenan."

"Kitty Clendenan? Is she that terribly plain young woman from the north country?"

"The very one! But she has a substantial inheritance, and, according to Alice, D'Arcy is penniless and in need of her income and so he has pledged his troth to her, publicly! This is devastating!"

For once, Emma had no idea what to do. Lizzie had conducted herself disgracefully with D'Arcy with the understanding that he was a man of means, and a man of his word. It now appeared he was neither. Emma stroked Lizzie's brow as she broke down on the floor in tears. The contrast between Emma's joy and Lizzie's misery was acute and no one was more aware of it than she. Despite her best efforts, she had no words of comfort for her sister.

Chapter 20. The Entourage

In the ensuing days, Emma informed her parents of Alberto's intentions and, although her father expressed some misgivings about the situation, her mother was delighted. Letter after letter appeared daily from Alberto with his plans for an English wedding, and his plans to buy the manor house that had belonged to the Dowager Duchess of Kent, just two miles away.

Finally, she received a letter announcing his travel plans. He begged to be allowed to stay there with his mother and their entourage. Consulting her father, Emma responded with glee that they were, of course, welcome! And only two weeks later, at the height of August, the Zobenigo son and his valet arrived with his mother and her lady's maid. It was late afternoon when their carriage pulled into the courtyard.

Emma ran to the courtyard to welcome her fiancé and his mother.

"Oh Alberto, you have come!" she cried.

Leaping from the carriage with incredible agility, Alberto took her in his arms and embraced her, and then, with some ceremony, he presented his mother, Barbara Zobenigo.

"My darling Emma, please allow me to present my mother, Barbara Zobenigo, who has come to oversee the plans for the wedding. She does not speak and English, but she is very good at planning large festivals, having done so for many of my cousins in Verona."

"I am very pleased to meet you Mrs. Zobenigo," said Emma with ceremony. "Sono molto onorato di fare la tua conoscenza, signora Zobenigo.[12]"

Emma's attempt to relate to Barbara Zobenigo was met with great joy by Alberto's mother. A sudden flurry of incomprehensible Italian spilled forth from her joy-filled lips. Emma, panicked, looked for help, to Alberto, but he was talking in

---

[12] I am honored to make your acquaintance, Mrs. Zobenigo.

rapid-fire Italian to his valet, and Emma realized she was trapped trying to understand what Barbara Zobenigo was saying. Fortunately for Emma, her mother, Anne, appeared, curious about the turmoil in the courtyard. She approached Barbara with a smile on her face, and without Emma, whose back was to her, knowing.

"Welcome to Godington Manor, Madama Zobenigo," she said in flawless Italian. Madama Zobenigo, doubtless relieved, turned to Anne Shaftesbury, and said: "You must be the matriarch of this august clan. I am very honored to join our family with yours. Your daughter fooled me with her one flawless sentence of welcome. I realize she speaks very little Italian. I must begin to learn your language too if we are to get along."

"Emma is very good with languages," said Anne. "She is very fluent in French and has only just begun, under my tutelage, to learn the Italian tongue."

"Ah!" said Barbara Zobenigo. "I, too, speak excellent French. We shall have a Tower of Babel here if we are not careful. I shall speak French to Emma." She said this sentence in French, and Emma, who finally understood, responded warmly.

"Thank God we can communicate with a common language," said Emma in French. "For I want to learn all about your son. I trust he is not fluent in French?"

"Oh no. He is the anglophile in the family. My son Domenico is the Francophile. In fact, Domenico is at this very moment living in Paris and studying at the Sorbonne. It is with his help that Alberto was able to purchase the dress we have all heard so much about. Will it be your wedding dress?"

"Indeed it shall," said Emma. "It is my prize possession."

"Well, that is wonderful. But please, let me know where my maid and the valet can deposit the trunks."

Later in the day, Alberto knocked shyly on Emma's bed chamber door, and, although he was not admitted into her chambers, she met him at the door and suggested they walk in the garden, as it was a delightful day.

"My mother wants to thank your family for their hospitality, and to that end, we have brought some delicacies from Italy. Her maid, Maria, is an excellent cook and would like to have leave to prepare you a typical Italian meal."

"That is my mother's area of expertise," said Emma. "I'm afraid I have no culinary skills at all, not even in organizing them. I have eaten many meals but never planned a single one."

"How charming!" enthused Alberto. "I shall ask your mother about that."

Walking through the well-tended garden, they admired the designs, with its trellises, fountains, and flower beds. Alberto was most interested in the market garden used by the cook.

"I have never known a farm to be incorporated into a beautiful and decorative garden," he remarked. "Most ingenious!"

For the evening meal, the turmoil caused by Maria, the unilingual Italian maid, in making the Italian delicacies, was nowhere on display. Despite the mayhem going on below the stairs, all appeared calm and pleasant in the large formal dining room.

First, the servants brought out what they called "a typical Italian soup" called Milanese Minestrone, which was a beautiful and delicious combination of vegetables in a lovely light broth. All the family were mightily impressed by this soup.

"It seems the Italians have a way of turning sow's ears into silk purses," declared Sir Rufus. Everyone was amused by his wit, particularly when the dull-witted Sebastian pulled a piece of pasta from his soup declaring: "Look papa, it appears as though they have left in the sow's ear after all."

Emma, as usual, was embarrassed by her foolish brother, but smiled despite her feelings because she was so happy her dreams were coming true. She squeezed Alberto's hand under the table, and he smiled at her with that beautiful, white-toothed grin she had come to admire so much.

The next dish was the one that perplexed all the English. "It is called Spaghetti Bolognese," explained Alberto. "It is said that this pasta, as we call it, was brought by the great traveler Marco Polo to Venice from the Orient. We serve it with a typical Italian tomato-based sauce," he said, to the gasps of Elizabeth and Anne; the English consider the tomato of "love apple" to be an aphrodisiac, and so they were scandalized.

"And so, these ropes or strings are called spaghetti?" asked Sir Rufus, looking perplexed at what to do.

"Yes," said Alberto. "As you can see, it is very simple, but takes a certain agility." While the Italians ate this delicacy with ease, twirling the ropes around their forks, the English were perplexed, not having the slightest idea how to eat this new foodstuff. They whirled and twirled the substance around, causing no end of spillage and stains on their attire. For minutes, they toiled, desperately trying not to look foolish while the Italians ate with relish, unaware of the distress of the Englishmen. In the end, it became a jolly affair, with all laughing at their ineptitude, and merriment was had by all.

  The dessert was a wonder as well, but not so alien to them. It was called cannoli and was a shell made of sweetened wheat, baked in an oven and filled with some sort of custard. The Italians had coated the top with chocolate, one of the most prized tastes in the entire English palette.

  Following dinner, Alberto had a conference with Sir Rufus in the smoking room. It appeared to be a solemn affair from Emma's perspective, but within minutes, the two gentlemen came to the ladies' sewing room to give the official announcement that an agreement had been struck. Alberto would wed Emma in England and Sir Rufus would assist in the purchase of the manor vacated by the dowager Duchess of Kent by vouching for his good character. Drinks were shared, and merriment was had by all. Sir Rufus introduced Port to the Italians, declaring, "you may have the most delicious food in the world but we cannot be matched with our drink!"

"I am overwhelmed, I confess," said Emma. "How on earth can you purchase that huge estate?"

"Well, Emma, your father will vouch for me, but, my love, I hope you shan't be upset, for I am heir to a considerable fortune from my family. It is more than simply considerable; it is monumental. I did not mention it earlier as it can be a topic of some difficulty, but you shall never want for anything again as long as you live. My income is somewhere in the area of twenty-five thousand of your guineas per year. I hope this does not upset you."

Emma, who had no idea of his wealth, was at first stunned. Elizabeth was agog and began laughing with her mouth open.

"Lizzie!" said Anne sternly. "Your manners!" But Lizzie was overwhelmed just as much as Emma was, for neither of them had the slightest inkling that Alberto was so wealthy. One of the hazards of wedding a foreigner is that you can never know their family or the family's station.

"I beg your family's indulgence, Sir Rufus, for I expect my father and my younger brother to arrive tomorrow. I will tell them to join us here so the whole family can begin to plan the festivities. I trust you can put up with them."

"Indubitably," said Sir Rufus. "If they are as delightful as you and your mother, they will be most welcome!"

Chapter 21. The Wedding

The plans for the wedding went quickly, and Sir Rufus had the invitations in the mail by the end of the week. Everything was passing in a blur for Emma, who spent her days trying on her beautiful dress and playing the pianoforte, or walking in the garden with her beloved Alberto. He was, in fact, nothing like Federico. He was a kind and thoughtful man, beautiful to behold in his elegant English clothes, and delightful in every way.

His brother, Domenico, arrived with the patriarch, Pietro-Paolo Zobenigo, the following day, and the two of them were housed in the guest rooms at the back of the manor. Pietro-Paolo and Barbara both spoke beautiful French and so it was agreed that the language would be French. Everyone but Alberto, who spoke English and Italian only, could communicate, with Emma translating for him.

"Emma, my love, can we visit the manor house of the dowager Duchess of Kent?" asked Alberto one morning.

"Of course," said Emma, delighted at the prospect of seeing her new home. The two of them went by hack with Pietro-Paolo and Sir Rufus the next day. As they arrived, there was an estate agent, a young and foppish fellow named Alistair Craven. He was impressed with the family and their obvious wealth. Nothing had been touched in the place since the demise of the dowager Duchess two years before and entering this place was a gloomy and strange affair. Ghostly white sheets covered much of the furniture which, although of good quality, was desperately ancient in style. Much of the furniture appeared to be pre-French Revolution pieces, of great beauty and frightfully ornate. The current style for everything was simple and elegant, and this ancient stuff was off-putting for poor Emma.

"Oh dear, Alberto. Do you think we need to have this old stuffy furniture?"

"Of course not," he said smiling. "Papa," he said, turning to his father, and speaking in Italian. "Do you think this furniture could be burned in a huge bonfire? We can call it our bonfire of the vanities!"

His father was scandalized by this characterization, invoking as it did an ancient embarrassing historical detail about Italy, the reign of the mad cleric Girolamo Savonarola who had burned hundreds of priceless books, paintings, and other art treasures, looked askance at his son.

"Alberto, this is no laughing matter," he said in Italian, so that Emma did not understand. "We can buy you new furniture, of course. In fact, I think a journey to London would be a good idea. What do you think?"

Emma was moved by this gesture of kindness, when Alberto translated for her. "Thank you very much father," she said to Pietro-Paolo.

The following day, the three of them set off with Nell to London to shop for new furniture. There were many shops they visited and hundreds of new pieces were purchased, set to be delivered a few days later. When the items arrived, Anne and Emma stayed at the new manor, organizing the new furniture. In a matter of three days, the house looked almost like a different place. Anne had organized a crew to remove the old furniture and move it to their London home, and then she corralled an army of craftsmen to paint the ceilings, paper the walls with new wallpaper, and carpets. The floors of hardwood were polished to a shine and the floors that were tiled with the terracotta tiling were washed carefully. By the time the evening of the fourth day arrived, the house was a home.

"I do believe we should have the wedding here!" said Elizabeth in joy.

"Pish tosh!" said Anne. "This garden will take years of tending. It has been set at our house and so it will be done." she was adamant, and for good reason, for the garden was overgrown and wild, inappropriate for a wedding.

On the day of the wedding, the entire Zobenigo family had decamped to the *Baying Hounds Inn,* so as not to see the bride in her finery. Emma was dressed by Nell, and looked beautiful. Her hair was pulled up in a chignon, jewels glittered through her hair, and she wore a diamond encrusted necklace with a sapphire pendant given to her by her mother. Her shoes were delicate slippers, and the gown! Oh, the gown was magnificent! When she made an entrance into the ballroom, where all the guests were congregated, there was a gasp as she was spotted for the first time. Her eyes shone like diamonds too and she had a veil covering her head made of fine lace.

Alberto, clad in a beautiful and finely-fitted English frock coat with trousers in the new fashion, looked more handsome than Emma had ever seen him. He was tall, thin, and stately, his shoulders broad, his waist narrow. He was a powerful man and he looked at her with a look of utter devotion.

He moved toward her as she slowly walked through the crowd. He lifted his right hand and put it ahead of him, to catch her hand should she need it.

They met in the middle of the dance floor, and he embraced her in a manner that Emma would have thought was scandalous but for the fact that the Bishop of Kent was in attendance, watching with admiration at the lovely couple. He had insisted Alberto take a long indoctrination into the Church of England, discovering, to his delight, that Alberto had done his homework and was thoroughly acquainted with the rites and the institutions of the Church. He was happy to welcome not only him but their entire family.

Domenico, the younger brother, a similarly tall and thin man of twenty-two, had spent most of his time trying to woo Elizabeth who was still stewing about that cad, D'Arcy Hamilton, and when she saw D'Arcy appear on the guest list, she was horrified, protesting to her mother that he had humiliated her.

Anne, knowing the way these things work, disregarded the protestation of Elizabeth, knowing the charms of the young Italian would eclipse this worry, ignored her, and welcomed D'Arcy Hamilton to their house on the day of the wedding. After all, she reasoned, he was close friends with Alberto Zobenigo and that was reason enough to include him.

When he entered the room, Elizabeth was deep in conversation with Domenico, and did not even notice D'Arcy's appearance. This satisfied Anne, who then turned her attention to her eldest daughter, who was clutching her husband-to-be in a delightful embrace.

The wedding went off without a hitch, according to the tradition of the Anglican Rite, and within an hour, the music played for them to recess to the garden, and all went perfectly.

The garden was the perfect backdrop for the joyous wedding celebration, and within an hour, the bride and groom were sitting in an especially-fitted coach, ready to go to their new home, two miles down the road. The assembled guests waved and smiled as the coach drove away down the road and inside, Emma looked at her husband for the first time.

"I suppose every happy bride says this feels like a dream, but I honestly cannot imagine that I am so happy. I want to know what I have done to deserve such a man as you, my dear Alberto."

"I was about to ask you the same question, Emma," he said. "But I know my passion is burning like a furnace at this moment and your beauty is fanning the flames of my desire. I hope I do not offend you when I tell you I want to take you right now!"

Emma laughed a crystal tinkling laugh and reached out to Alberto, stroking his leg from the knee to the thigh. He smiled broadly, and clapped his large hand on her small one. He put his other hand to her shoulder, and smiled.

"What do you think? It is blessed by the bishop himself!" He laughed.

Emma, finally freed of all the trappings of propriety, felt the scales fall from her eyes and she saw the animal lust of Alberto as a power she wanted, that she wanted to own, to possess, to have acting on her. Without thinking, Emma rose and sat beside him so the two of them were sitting together on the seat, facing forward. She raised the hem of her skirt above her ankle and watched his face as it turned red from his neck and through his jaw, and then to his cheeks. At the same time that the redness began to fill him with embarrassment, his smile became wider and lustier.

Nevertheless, and despite his worldliness, he was loath to take liberties with her.

"May I?" he asked before placing a hand on her breast.

"You must," she murmured, as she felt the gentle rocking of the carriage. He smiled as he placed his hand tenderly on her breast, caressing gently, and for the first time in her life, Emma felt she was in the lead. She needed to instruct this older man in the ways of pleasure for herself.

Emma felt her hand run up the abdomen and chest of her husband. He had a very well-proportioned torso and she felt the need to unfasten each button from the neck to the navel. As it unbuttoned, she saw his smile turn to a look of wonder. He sat higher in his seat than before and, as his shirt tails were freed from his trousers, Emma she looked up at him over her long lashes, and smiled coquettishly.

He was blushing more and more with each moment she undressed him. Her hands, tiny and delicate, were strong and confident and making sure all things were being taken care of; Alberto had taken his larger and rougher hands, and placed them at her ankles, gently rising to her knee and when he reached her knee, he felt the bare skin where her silk stocking ended.

The moment when his fingers felt the bare skin, things about him began to change. From a frightened school boy to a soldier standing at attention, his demeanor changed and he suddenly knew the feeling of her tender and soft pale skin on the inside of her leg was an invitation as old as the love itself. He had never known this before and despite his worldly bearing, he was powerless against the onslaught of so much joy and desire.

He felt her move her leg so it rested on his. He felt her tiny hand as it unfastened the cummerbund around his waist, and she felt her lips on his chin. A kiss, from her tender and full red lips was placed slightly askew from his lip. He turned and put his arm around her back, which was draped in the beautiful golden material. However, as she had loosened the bodice, it was draping over her back, and exposing her neck and the top of her shapely back. The fact that he could see halfway down her back was immensely erotic for Alberto. He was far too shy to touch the beautiful back of course, but the sight of her exposed back was almost too much for Alberto to stand. She was busy unfastening his trousers and he was beginning to feel his emotions were getting the better of him when the coach suddenly came to a halt.

Neither of them was expecting this, having been carried away by their passion and the fact that they were alone for the first time ever. Emma looked out the window and saw that the coach had arrived at their manor. Embarrassed, she began to fasten her buttons again as the coachman leapt from the box to the ground. As his boots hit the ground, he straightened up and grasped the door handle, pulling it open. Emma had not counted on this happening and consequently when the door flew open, her décolletage was visible, not having been fastened properly. She door stood open and several servants were standing outside the door, as they do when the master returns home. They were likely not expecting to see quite so much of either the master or the mistress though, and all of them made great efforts to conceal their embarrassment.

In the manor, the rooms had been cleaned and swept so they were beautiful and sparkling with newness. The couple began mounting the stairs to the master bedroom. Halfway up the stairs, at the first landing, Alberto looked at Emma, and smiled, his right eyebrow raising and his face reddened slightly. She looked back at him, quizzically, knowing by his look that something was afoot. Although the only sound that could be heard in the house was the ticking of the grandfather clock they had purchased in London, the scene seemed to take on a musical soundtrack of its own.

Rushing violins, surging 'cellos, pounding pianoforte chords, stentorian trumpets, plaintive oboes, and romantic flutes all came together in one rushing wind as Alberto gathered Emma in his arms and bore her up the remaining stairs, which he took two at a time. When he reached the closed door of the master bedroom, he kicked it open with his boot and charged in, depositing her gently on the bed. Then he tore off his boots, ripped the shirt from his body, exposing his powerful and heaving chest to her, and removed his trousers. With the smile of a conquering hero, he descended on her, his large hands grasping her bodice and literally tearing it from her heaving bosom.

"Alberto!" she sighed, as he embraced her roughly.

Gasping but totally unashamed, Emma grasped at her husband's chest, pulling him to her, and firmly grasping the firm flesh of his manhood, which grew firmer still with her touch. Tussling with Alberto, she felt him overpower her and as he did this, she fell backward on the bed, whereupon he leapt up and lifted her skirts.

His hands traced the line to her waist, stopping to taste the forbidden fruits between her legs. His kisses were complete, covering her from toes to her waist and every square inch in between.

She was unable to control herself and closed her beautiful blue eyes as his powerful body took her again and again in a long-awaited passionate love. He thrust into her with power and masculine energy, while she guided him almost expertly, having learned many months ago exactly where to create magic.

A flash of a warm bath and the beautiful sensations went by her mind but she tossed this memory aside, so she suddenly knew exactly what she, a modern and sensitive woman, needed from a man. She thought briefly about the silly and vapid mustachioed man she had thought she loved, and realized that impressions, exoticism and the thrill of being loved were nothing compared to the fulfillment she was now feeling. The physical feelings of joy and excitement blossomed with each thrust Alberto made, and the joy of knowing how passionate and truthful he was were thanks for being steadfast and honest to herself. She knew, and would never forget, that he was the man who completed her life in exactly the same measure as she knew she completed his.

She lay back on the bed and smiled a smile so broad she could almost not imagine a better feeling. This was what life had in store for her, and she lay back to count her many blessings. She thought of the sadness endured by her sister Elizabeth and wished and prayed for happiness in equal measure for her. Her mother had told her about the sadness she had endured before she met her father, Sir Rufus, and so she knew her mother had not had the luxury of meeting a kindred spirit as she had.

"You are my life, Alberto," she murmured quietly, almost so quiet that she wondered if he had heard her.

"And you are my life," he said. The joy of hearing that sentence made her heart expand to a level she had never known before. It was as though the pain experienced by women for centuries had suddenly telescoped into her body and her joy had melted all of it away. Emma Shaftesbury was complete.

The End.

Made in the USA
Middletown, DE
22 July 2021